Much of Madness, More of Sin

A Collection

ANDREW WOLTER

ISBN-13 : 978-0-578-06103-0

First Trade Paperback Edition March 2011

Cover Art by Carl Craig

Published by:

Shadow City Press

16211 N. Scottsdale Road
Scottsdale, AZ 85254

Manufactured in the United States of America

Acknowledgements

As always, I am greatly appreciative to those of whom I have been honored to have in my life. I have seen loved ones come and go, but those of you who hold a warm light in your hearts for me, and understand the chaos that comes with the world of writing, it is to you that I extend a special thanks for your patience and undying love.

Then there are those who have been a part of my life for as long as I can remember. I thank the following people for always being there for me throughout the years: Stacy LaSalle, Suzanne Ziemer, Melissa Troyer, Sabrina Troyer and Gregory Cook.

To my mom, thanks for being the inspiration that has allowed me to arrive at this point in my career. And to the rest of my family of whom I extend my deepest gratitude—Darrell, Olga, Rudy (RuRu), Deandra, Nicole, Joseph, Alex, Dawn, Dacota, Rob, Niki, Chuy, Chad, and Anthony Michael Joaquin.

A major shout out goes to Carl Craig for seeing my vision of the cover for this collection. You're talent is amazing and I appreciate the time you put into this project.

The particular acknowledgments for this collection wouldn't be complete without stating to Rusty, Carlos, and Steven that there is a dark place in my heart that will always vaguely burn for each and every one of you.

Also by Andrew Wolter

Nightfall

To the memory of love and ashes of lust.

Much of Madness, More of Sin

Table of Contents

And Horror the Soul of the Plot: A Foreword.....................................Page 11

The Feast of Bacchus...Page 15

Jailed...Page 29

If Not For Death...Page 43

Everlong..Page 59

Being Human..Page 65

In the Shadow of Hades...Page 77

The Baths at the End of the Road..Page 89

Trick of Fate..Page 103

Joseph's Request...Page 121

A Cub's Tail...Page 135

Much of Madness, More of Sin...Page 145

...And Horror the Soul
of the Plot
A Foreword to *Much of Madness, More of Sin*

The title of this foreword refers to a line from Edgar Allan Poe's poem *The Conqueror Worm*. This particular work of Poe's can easily be interpreted as human life being full with dramatic recklessness that ultimately ends in gruesome demise. It suggests that man is blinded by his own daily commotion to a universe ruled by sinister forces.

As a populace predominantly starstruck by beauty, money, love, and sex, it comes as no surprise that we would develop tunnel vision to the phantasma we limit to our nightmares. After all, wouldn't we rather identify with a world in which happy endings are abundant; a surrounding in which success and pleasure create a life without worry? Or would we rather dwell on that which is unknown to us; that which could endanger everything for which we worked so hard to achieve? Perhaps it is our daily routines that pose the biggest threat, as we neglect the unknown by which we are surrounded. How do we know if a hideous being may be using that ravishing stranger at the bar as a host for its evil doing? What happens to our true love that has violently passed and continues to hold on to the world of the living? How do we recognize the face of a friend who possesses such a jealous rage that he or she is willing to wake an underworld?

The tales within *Much of Madness, More of Sin* incorporate a modern reality centered on graphic terror and ultimate lust. When one thinks of madness, it is commonly suggestive of insanity or inexplicable terror. Of sin, many are reminded that both wrath and lust are common when discussing the immorality of Man from the point of view of Christianity.

My main objective for this collection was to take madness and sin to the next level, a place in which the boundaries are pushed into a world that is unapologetic. I longed to discover what was truly *much* of madness and *more* of sin. In my experiences, I realized that the reality of love and loss was at the forefront of these subjects. It was from this concept, that the stories within this collection were born.

Because of this, I anticipate some critics referring to the tales within this collection as "shock fiction." The purpose of these tales is not to push the proverbial envelope; rather, I wanted to develop these stories without having to hold back for the sake of those who may find them immoral, gory, or pornographic. Yes, readers can expect graphic scenes of lust. Surely, there are disturbing scenes that may have stomachs churning. Most importantly, the element of horror remains at the core of each and every one of the tales contained within this collection.

One of my favorite things about the writing process is the development of characters within the story. I've always been a firm believer in emotional characterization. Although there are those who would establish that such sentiments may be lacking from a collection in which sex and death are prominent, I can assure you that the characterization within these tales is the driving force of each plot.

As a gay man, many of the characters within my stories reflect the pop-culture incorporated within the gay male figure. However, the characters in *Much of Madness, More of Sin* are as real as any other human. They live, eat, breathe, cry, laugh, work, manipulate, and fuck. Some are wounded from a love lost, while others seek absolution for their secret crimes. Some work corporate jobs and live comfortably, while others monetarily struggle from one night to the next as male hustlers. While the characters within this collection come from all walks of life, they share the same desire to seek out something more, in hopes of improving their current circumstances. It is these characters with which I'm certain you will easily identify.

As a writer, my goal has always been to move a person with my prose. Whether the stories that follow cause your hair to stand on end, have you running to the toilet to regurgitate, or even get you slightly aroused, then I will be satisfied in knowing that I have accomplished what I set out to do.

As the reader who has purchased this book, I urge you to approach these stories with an open mind. The imagination of an author should never be limited to the boundaries of a society that tends to preach what is or isn't ethical while, at the same time, obsessing over their beauty, greedily spending money on the latest designer clothing, and engaging in casual sex with strangers met in a bar two hours previous to their arrival. Thus, the tales within this collection are without limit.

Although the stories contained within cross over into graphic and gratuitous circumstances that surpass the content of my normal prose, and because of the particular theme of *Much of Madness, More of Sin*, I have created eleven original tales never before published. Yet, through the controversial story lines, readers can expect to find a message in each tale. And, yes, horror is at the soul of the plot!

I hope that you enjoy the story lines, creatures, and characters within this collection as much as I did while creating them.

Andrew Wolter
Phoenix, Arizona
December 2010

* * *

"That motley drama- oh, be sure
It shall not be forgot!
With its Phantom chased for evermore,
By a crowd that seize it not,
Through a circle that ever returneth in
To the self-same spot,
And much of Madness, and more of Sin,
And Horror the soul of the plot."

–Edgar Allan Poe, *The Conqueror Worm*

The Feast of Bacchus

I. The Days of Bacchus

It would be the last day the monsters could roam free throughout the streets of downtown Phoenix. However, they weren't the kind of monsters kids feared when they trembled in their beds and kept a watchful eye on a closet door slightly ajar. They were not creatures of myth, hell-bent on draining the blood of their victims or morphing into mouth-watering beasts by the light of a full moon. They were neither immortal nor did they possess supernatural powers. Instead, they were humans in disguise, donning the masks of creatures.

Given the marching groups of costumed men and women that made their way down Central Avenue, one may have easily confused the date for Halloween. However, the springtime sun shone down upon the glistening asphalt and the temperature had reached a comforting eighty degrees. It was the second week in April, and it was the final day commemorating the celebration of the Days of Bacchus.

The Days of Bacchus was not a widely celebrated event. In fact, its observation was primarily noted by the twenty-something "artsy" crowd. It had begun nine years previous as a night in honor of the Roman god known as Bacchus—the patron deity of agriculture and theatre. A local theatre group, located in the heart of downtown Phoenix, had devoted an evening honoring theatre and the independent arts. The turnout for the event was phenomenal and brought more culture, along with people, to the otherwise corporate-oriented downtown area. It had only been a matter of time before the mom and pop delis, the independently owned coffee houses, and a number of other locally owned businesses on the brink of closing their doors joined the cause.

Within a couple of years, the celebration became a week of days and nights in which local artists of all walks of life—musicians, sculptors, poets, and stage actors—were honored. Every second week of April, the executives who donned power suits to the downtown high rises made of glass and steel were subjected to the parades of young partiers dressed in costume. To some, it was a freakshow and, to others, it was a distraction to the life of stocks and business, of power and wealth. Yet, the small business owners of Phoenix found it to be prosperous, as the stampede of monsters would always frequent the local shops and eateries. The Days of Bacchus brought notoriety to the city's otherwise unknown artists—local musicians acquired small-label record deals from gigs played during The Days of Bacchus; starving artists sold pieces to San Francisco galleries from art shows featured during The Days of Bacchus; and stage actors were invited to Broadway auditions from plays performed during The Days of Bacchus.

In Roman mythology, Bacchus was also known as the Liberator, freeing one from one's normal self, by madness, ecstasy, or wine. These long forgotten tales created the image that became The Days of Bacchus. The tribute to this mythos had young crowds parading the downtown area wearing gruesome face paints and latex masks. They carried goblets of wine—some filled with red merlots to match their bloody-colored faces and others with white chardonnays to blend with the painted diamond-like sparkles that adorned their bodies.

Jeremy watched the carnival of costumes, observing the way the altered human conditions had no respect for those not taking part in the celebration. He shook his head as he studied a small group walk against a stoplight. A blaring horn scolded them and, in return, three from the crowd obscenely gestured with their middle fingers.

"Fuck," Jeremy said beneath his breath.

He was glad at the thought of today being the final in The Days of Bacchus celebration. Although he always had a great time hanging out with his best friend, Zeke, the festivities hurt his business more so than not. After all, the police were in full force during the celebration. What rational man would come looking for a good time with all those cops in their overpriced SUV's, not to mention the ones riding on horseback through the downtown blocks?

Jeremy's cell phone rang. The text upon the LCD screen announced it was Zeke.

"Hey," he casually answered. Jeremy winced as he immediately pulled the phone from his ear. It sounded as if a train of screaming passengers was about to fly off the tracks and lead them to a treacherous death. Jeremy barely made out Zeke's high-pitched voice.

"I'm near Washington and Central," Jeremy said. "Where are you? Why is it so fucking loud?" *Shit*, Jeremy thought. He had completely forgotten that he was supposed to meet Zeke at the Hellfire concert. He wasn't sure what to say to Zeke and didn't want to hurt his feelings for not showing up.

Jeremy could hear the echo of *BAH-CUS* repeat from the other end of the line. "I'm sorry, dude," he spoke into the receiver. *BAH-CUS...BAH-CUS...BAH-CUS.* "Zeke? Zeke, are you there?" Jeremy yelled. "Who? The three of who? I can't understand you. Licking your neck?" Jeremy was getting frustrated and forcefully rubbed his forehead. Zeke could've at least had enough courtesy to leave the theatre to finish the conversation. "Hello? HELLO?" There was no way Zeke could have heard him, what with the sounds of the drums beating to the rhythm of fans screaming, "BAH-CUS."

A loud crack made its way into Jeremy's ear. He listened as the audience carried on. "ZEKE?"

Soon, he heard Zeke's voice. It seemed hollow and distant, as if it at the other end of a tunnel. The only words he could understand were that of a series of screeches above the cheering crowds. The screams he heard tied his stomach in knots and caused a threatening tightness in his chest. "...biting me...help...Jeremy...he's eating meeeeeeeee!"

"What the fuck?" Jeremy hung up and re-dialed Zeke's number. Four rings later, he was greeted by Zeke's voicemail. "Hey, it's Zeke. Now that you got me, whatcha gonna do to me?"

Jeremy didn't bother leaving a message. It was all plain as day. Zeke was obviously playing another one of his jokes. *Jealous bitch,* Jeremy mentally scolded.

It was no surprise that Zeke adored Jeremy. In fact, he had tried hitting on Jeremy more than once and had always suggested threesomes as a way to get them together in the same room. The stunt he'd just pulled was another in a series of trying to get him to go where he was. In this case, the Hellfire concert. Well, Jeremy wasn't the jealous type and it wouldn't work. In one way, Jeremy was pained by guilt for not meeting up with him. Then again, Zeke had been very clingy in the past six months. Not to mention, Jeremy had to distance himself from Zeke. If he was going to set his plan in motion, he had to cut ties with everything that was a part of what would become *that* life.

"Hey," a voice called.

Jeremy turned and was greeted by a balding man in his forties with thick bifocals. His paranoid gesture of glancing up and down the street blew his would-be innocent cover. Jeremy strutted toward the sedan. "What's up?"

"You working?" The man's eyes were wide and hungry. He anxiously licked his lips.

"Of course," Jeremy grinned.

"You a cop?" the stranger asked.

Jeremy laughed. "What do you think? Pull near the alley and I'll meet you there."

II. Hellfire Takes the Stage

Bellowing screams flooded the atmosphere of the Dodge Theatre as the luster of overhead lights softly dimmed. It was the last opportunity the riotous crowd had to observe those around them and the various costumed faces decorated with multi-colored paints, covered by latex masks, and drooling from rank alcohol mouths.

Zeke glanced back at either of the entrances that poured into the mouth of the Dodge Theatre. Although he'd wished his hopeful search would find Jeremy casually strolling into the theatre, he knew better. It wasn't even five o'clock. Surely, Jeremy was turning another trick.

Fuckin' figures, Zeke thought. And it didn't matter that this was the final night of the Days of Bacchus. It didn't matter that Hellfire was about to take the stage for one crazy ass show. What mattered was that Jeremy had promised him they would spend time together this evening—hang out, get high, have a fucking celebration unlike any other. That's what friends did!

The crowd exploded into a dynamic uproar as deep, crimson hues ignited the stage and four silhouettes came into focus. The shadowy figures proved to be the members of the local rock band, Hellfire. The undying din of the anxious fans looped over itself as one of the band members scurried behind the outline of a set of drums. Two of the three remaining members advanced to either side of the stage, picking up their guitars, leaving the voice of Hellfire (known as Felix Angst) standing alone in the center of the stage. Felix adjusted his stance to one that mimicked the shape of a standing pentagram—his legs spread wide and his arms raised high in the air. The screeching of fans ensued.

Amidst the throng of jumping followers who gave tribute to Hellfire, Zeke turned in search of Jeremy once again. The red tint that reflected from the stage lights made the observation across the sea of costumed faces murky at its best. The fetid smell of skunk weed infused his senses as he gazed at the rolling clouds of smoke captured by the blood-colored hues. It was no use; he wouldn't find Jeremy even if he had shown up.

Zeke reached into his pocket for his cell phone. As he pivoted his direction toward the stage, his shoulder bumped against a sparkling chest that was painted gold. For a moment, Zeke stared at the defined pectoral muscles of the figure—how pronounced; how statuesque! A hatchet-sharp face, the color of deep purple, met his upward glance and caused his heart to flutter. The Roman nose of the painted visage was prominent and strong, the line of his jawbone meticulously carved, and the tousled hair fell in wisps, framing the man's features. The irises of the stranger's eyes gleamed red, perhaps reflecting the tints of the stage lights. They reminded Zeke of the red contacts he'd purchased online last Halloween as part of his demon costume.

"I'm sorry," Zeke yelled his apology. He was unsure if the man heard him over the screeching teenagers next to them.

"Not a problem," the man announced in a thunderous baritone voice.

Beyond the purple lips, Zeke made out the fleshy pink colors within the man's mouth.

Zeke's gaze was torn away from the enigmatic stranger by the even beat of distant toms, courtesy of Hellfire's drummer. The sharp, hollow thuds alternated with a half-beat of silence in between. *Boom thud...boom thud...boom thud.*

Zeke took notice of Hellfire's front man who was now clapping overhead to the rhythm of the drumbeat. The audience joined in as Zeke flipped open his cell phone. He scrolled through the list of contacts until he found Jeremy's name, then clicked the green button upon the keypad to call his absent friend. From behind, Zeke felt the hand of the stranger he'd encountered graze the small of his back. His body uncontrollably trembled.

"Jeremy," Zeke yelled into the phone. "It's Zeke," he yelled. "Where are you?" A brief pause. "I'm at the Hellfire concert that you were supposed to meet me at; of course it's fucking loud!"

Zeke's bitching came to an abrupt halt as a subtle heat pierced the back of his neck. It was followed by the felt touch of delicate lips. Zeke took a deep, invigorating breath through his nose.

"BAH-CUS," the singer of Hellfire roared into the microphone and flooded the wailing screams of two thousand fans. "BAH-CUS...BAH-CUS...BAH-CUS." The cadence of Felix Angst's voice matched the beat of the drummer's *boom thud*. Soon, the audience joined in with clapping hands that kept time and shouts of "BAH-CUS...BAH-CUS...BAH-CUS."

"Yeah, I'm here," Zeke hollered into the phone after being caught off guard by the advances made by the strange man from behind. "Dude, you SO have to be here! There's this hot guy. The three of us totally have to get together! I said the three of us —"

Zeke's conversation was immediately interrupted by the fleshy, moist sensation of the stranger's tongue licking the nape of his neck. His heart burst into a gallop and giddiness infiltrated his stomach. He thought he was going to get a hard-on right there.

"BAH-CUS...BAH-CUS...BAH-CUS..."

"Dude, he's licking my neck," he shouted into the phone. "Licking my neck," he repeated.

The open space between Zeke and the colorfully painted man behind him closed as he felt his back being pulled against the stranger's burly chest. A tingling sensation infused Zeke's entire body as if a tickling from a low-voltage electric shock. Zeke continued holding the phone to his ear, trying to hear Jeremy's voice, and began swaying with the lovable stranger to the intonations that permeated the theatre.

"BAH-CUS...BAH-CUS...BAH-CUS..."

Zeke winced from the piercing pinch upon his neck. Within seconds, he felt the same sharp nips to both shoulders. Before Zeke had the opportunity to turn, he felt what seemed to be a slow razor slice to the back of his neck. The phone dropped from his hand as he tried to turn around. An uneven agony traveled along either side of his neck and met at his forehead. Zeke's head began to feel numb and his vision blurred. His head bobbed back and forth as if he were floating upon a sea of waves. His heart erupted into a quickening thud that brought tension to his throat. As he gasped for air, Zeke realized the man behind him was chewing upon the back of his neck. With each jog of the head, Zeke felt the man's teeth dig deeper, hitting nerves and sending intense flares that jolted the gray matter of his brain.

Zeke screeched, unable to break from the stranger's strong hold. He shrieked, in hopes that Jeremy would hear him. "He's biting me! Help! Jeremy...he's eating meeeeeee!"

A minute later, the electric blue glow of an incoming call brightened the screen of Zeke's cell phone. It would go unnoticed beneath the feet of the excited fans within the Dodge Theatre.

Nearby, Zeke faced the stranger with whom he had earlier met. His body wavered back and forth, as if it were in an undying trance. Zeke sleepily stared into the red eyes of his assailant. Had his vision been unhampered, he would have seen the bloody colors of the stranger's eyes effortlessly swirl like whirlpools. Had Zeke not been within his unnatural trance, he would have noticed his flesh that stained the stranger's perfect teeth pink. But all that Zeke noticed were the liquid waves of purple oceans that had become his solitude.

"BAH-CUS...BAH-CUS...BAH-CUS..."

"Days of Bacchus, Phoenix," yelled Felix Angst. "Are you ready to party?"

The energetic, bellowing screams eclipsed all the simple sounds within the Dodge Theatre, whether it the ringtone of a cell phone or a man pleading for his life.

III. Resignation

A group of laughing monsters greeted Jeremy as he exited the alley. The crowd practically whisked him off balance, temporarily forcing him to move along with the troupe that excitedly marched down Central Avenue.

With as much ease with which the parade had swept him away, Jeremy broke from the crowd and walked in the opposite direction. He wiped at the corner of his mouth, trying to erase the awful taste of the man from the alley. The stranger's mouth had taste like the rancid pine flavor of a cheap gin. His cum was bitter and metallic, practically caustic. Jeremy reached into the front of his Levi 501's and made sure the crumpled twenty-dollar bill was still there.

Between Washington Street and Van Buren Avenue, Jeremy brought his stride back to his motel room to a halt. The mirrored glass of the Phoenix Esrever tower reflected blinding, orange rays from a setting sun upon the western horizon. Jeremy winced, and then shielded his eyes from the sharp light. The corporate building was one of the tallest within the glass and stucco city, second to the Chase Bank building that towered Phoenix and boasted an American flag from its zenith.

Jeremy observed the throng of young men that exited from the revolving, glass door of the skyscraper. Those men—sporting Gucci and Armani suits along with short-cropped hair that was styled with designer gels and forming creams—how he admired them! Look at the way they talk amongst themselves as if they elite, as if nothing else mattered in the world save for their corporate status and the Vaio laptops encased within Prada satchels sleekly slung over their shoulders. Surely, they were heading to the parking garage where they would get behind the wheel of a new Audi, BMW, or Jaguar and then head home to a luxury condo or townhouse.

Jeremy sighed and lowered his head, ashamed of viewing such successful men of working society. His stomach quivered with anxiety fueled by embarrassment. *Should've quit this business long ago*, he thought. *Should've quit last night.*

Indeed, that was Jeremy's initial plan: to quit the night before. After all, he had saved enough money for first and last month's rent (along with a security deposit) for a real apartment. Even the small confines of a studio would prove better than the run-down motel room from which he'd been living the past year and a half. What's more, Jeremy was tired of using his body to make money, disgusted by ways with which he received an extra twenty to save toward achieving a better life. Thinking of such sexually vile acts worried Jeremy to no end. Perhaps, this differentiated him from the other whores who walked the turf of downtown Central Avenue.

Sure, Jeremy knew that the life of a male prostitute was full of risk. The more money one wanted to make was not only dictated by the wildest fantasy of a desperate *john*, but by the degree of risk with which the hustler was willing to accept. Jeremy had fraternized with many of the other *rentboys* in the area. In fact, that was how he'd first met Zeke. Within the year and a half he sold his mouth and ass on the streets, he realized a majority of the others were no longer around; their faces were nothing but latex memories stretched with lines that defined their age as being much older than they truly were. He had heard those young men, excited to get a fifty-dollar bill for allowing their *john* to fuck them up the ass without a condom. Those same, once attractive youths had been horribly transformed into gaunt creatures, sickened by one or many diseases that came with the territory.

Jeremy had led this life. This was the world, both daring and unprotected, in which Jeremy existed. Still, Jeremy maintained his mindset that he was only a visitor to this dark bump upon the road of Life. He had a plan, yes! He stuck to his plan, refusing to give in to the all-night parties of which many of the other hustlers had become fixtures.

Jeremy's determination to stick to his goals paid off. The night before the final celebration of The Days of Bacchus, Jeremy made the decision to quit selling his body. He had saved up enough money and had several job interviews as a Customer Service Representative set up for the following week. He was going to emerge from this world of anonymous lovemaking and dangerous sexual fantasies. He planned to live the life of a normal American young man—a job, an apartment, and perhaps a relationship with a man with whom he would, for once, wake by his side when the sun came up. Just thinking of such things the average person usually took for granted had Jeremy's mind racing all night through the witching hour.

Then it hit him, a realization that he couldn't deny. The final night of The Days of Bacchus! It was a night of illusion, a population in costume and hiding who they truly were. It would be a night without inhibitions to those who were too embarrassed to show their face as they engaged in sex with a stranger. Jeremy recalled the previous year, a night in which he'd made almost three hundred dollars. Why not add that extra bonus to the funds with which he had already saved? It made perfect sense to him. Thus, Jeremy made his way out onto the dusky street of Phoenix for one final night.

A teenager with a smiling ghost face bumped into Jeremy and detached him from his reverie. "Sorry, dog," the youth hollered back. The happy phantom was accompanied by three blood-splattered princesses and two others dressed to look like Frankenstein's monster and a werewolf. *How cute*, he thought. And it was the only time Jeremy could recall associating the word "cute" when faced by the visage of a monster. After all, Jeremy had seen real monsters in his life, creatures that didn't have to don a frightful mask to prove they were evil. The monsters in Jeremy's day-to-day life were those of everyday men with a concealed lust. They were men who left their wives and children to have their dicks sucked by a stranger in an alley for twenty bucks. They were the type of men who maintained a masculine, all-American quarterback facade to their rich college buddies and sorority girlfriend while they thrust their cocks into the ass of another man, during the midnight hour in n a seedy motel room. Yes, Jeremy knew such men as clients. But to a society where social stature dictates one's happiness, the power of a secret can easily divide the line between the actions of a respectable man and those of a degenerate.

Jeremy briskly studied his cell phone, checking to see if he'd missed a call from Zeke. The stranger he had serviced in the alley grunted so loud, he would have been unable to hear the soft chiming ringtone of his cell. Hell, Jeremy was shocked that the man's climatic bellows didn't draw more attention to the alley.

Jeremy glanced at the screen of his cell phone and began walking down Central Avenue, en route to his motel room. The skies above grew dim, and the combination of a vast setting sun and the low-hanging clouds created a deep purple like that of a fresh, deliciously juicy grape.

After walking less than three blocks, Jeremy noticed s gold Nissan Sentra pull alongside the curb and slow to a crawl. He began walking toward the vehicle and smiled as the passenger-side window eased down. The passenger's face was purple, his lips and eyes red. He was obviously in costume for the night's festivities.

"What's up?"

"Get in," the man nonchalantly directed. His voice was soothing and altogether inviting.

Jeremy kneeled by the passenger side door to get a closer at Purple-Face. "Whatcha looking to—" Jeremy observed the driver. "Zeke?"

Jeremy's friend casually turned his neck and faced him. Red paint spattered the back of his neck and either side of his head. His eyes veritably glowed with a red tint that Jeremy recognized from the specialty contacts Zeke had purchased last Halloween. Zeke's expressions were indifferent, but his eyes begged for company. Then he turned his attention toward the street that lay ahead.

"Don't even tell me you stole a fucking car!" Jeremy knew Zeke was fucked up on something beyond the shrooms they use to smoke from time to time. *Probably meth or GHB.* Jeremy quickly felt responsible for his friend. The guilt of not meeting him at the Hellfire concert didn't help matters.

With those thoughts in mind, Jeremy opened the back door and climbed into the car. "Drive to my motel room," he directed his friend. "Slowly."

As the car lurched forward, the clanking of bottles caught Jeremy's attention. "What's this?" he asked as he studied the inside a plastic grocery bag. "Wine? Seriously, you guys are taking this celebration a bit too literally."

"Tonight, there shall be a feast," the passenger stated.

IV. The Great Feast

The hollow pop of a wine cork interrupted the awkward silence between the three men.

Jeremy turned his attention from the bulging, gold-painted chest of the stranger to Zeke. He observed Zeke robotically grab a few glass tumblers from off the nightstand and pour merlot, evenly measuring the amount within each glass. He casually offered a glass to Jeremy, then handed one to the stranger.

Tension hung in the air like an invisible virus all around them. Jeremy felt a fluttering in his stomach. He broke the silence by asking, "So what are we drinking to?"

"To Bacchus," Zeke spoke.

"OK. To Bacchus."

The three men raised their glasses and pushed them together to form an echoing clank. Jeremy watched the quiet stranger consume the entire portion of wine in one rapid gulp. Quickly finishing his own glass, Zeke's hand reached out to take the tumbler from Jeremy.

Jeremy stood opposite of the purple-faced stranger. The man's eyes stared into his soul, and Jeremy soon felt as if he were being cradled upon a soothing ocean. Tightness formed in his chest; a lump swelled in his throat. Something wasn't right about the man. Something was off with the way in which Zeke had been acting.

From behind, Jeremy felt Zeke's arms come around and embrace him. He felt the soft kisses and subtle licks upon his neck. Jeremy briskly turned toward his friend.

"Stop! What are you doing?"

Zeke's eyes were as innocent as his answer. "We want to be with you."

"Dude, you know I don't mess around with you."

Zeke ignored Jeremy altogether and planted his mouth on Jeremy's lips. He began pushing his tongue into Jeremy's mouth. Jeremy pulled back, placing his hand upon Zeke's shoulder to create distance. "What the fuck's wrong with you?"

"It's not him," a smooth voice emitted from behind Jeremy.

Jeremy spun toward the stranger and observed the space between them close.

"What are you talking about? Who are you?" asked Jeremy.

The guest placed his large hands upon Jeremy's shoulders and looked him dead in the eyes. "I am Bacchus. This is the final night of my feast."

Jeremy attempted to speak, but found himself without a voice.

"It's not Zeke you want. You want me."

Jeremy violently shook his head. His stomach folded and he thought he was going to vomit.

The man named Bacchus gestured toward Zeke with his eyes of swirling red. "That's not even Zeke. Zeke's been dead for a while. That's simply my puppet."

At that, Jeremy could hear the weight of Zeke's body instantly hit the carpet of the room.

"Your resistance is useless, Jeremy." Bacchus' eyes met with Jeremy's emerald irises. "You should be filled with pride, with satisfaction, that you will be the final feast of the year. Surely, you will become a martyr."

No! God, no! Jeremy mentally screeched. He heard the heavy thuds of his heart in his ears, practically eclipsing the voice of the man in front of him. His body uncontrollably trembled as if he were going into an epileptic fit. He was unable to will any movement in his frame of flesh, as if he frozen in a nightmarish trance.

Bacchus brought his hands to either side of Jeremy's face. He slowly moved in and placed his purple mouth over Jeremy's, sucking in Jeremy's lips. Pulling back, he gently bit Jeremy's lower lip. Then, without any hesitation, Bacchus opened his mouth and bit down hard. With teeth fiercely clenched, he pulled on Jeremy's lower lip until a small chunk ripped from his mouth.

The flare of both instant pain and numbing agony infused Jeremy's entire body. He felt the liquid warmth of blood rushing down his chin and neck. If only to scream! If only to run from this horrifying reality, this nightmare fantastic! Instead, all Jeremy could do was shudder as he watched Bacchus excitedly chew the flesh of his lip as if it were an appetizing treat.

Bacchus violently grasped at Jeremy's t-shirt and ripped it off in one quick tear. He fiercely tugged the young man's jeans to his ankles.

Jeremy felt the warmth from his wound tickle his stomach and seep into his crotch.

Bacchus pulled down his own pants, and Jeremy's eyes bulged at the sight of the lengthy, serpentine organ that swayed back and forth as if it a cobra summoned from its wicker lair. The young man's shoulders tensed and he thought he felt a micro-explosion is his chest as he watched the head of Bacchus' cock sway upward. The hole at the tip opened and revealed dozens of miniature, jagged teeth that continuously grinded against each other.

A throaty laughter emitted from Bacchus' mouth.

With eyes widened, Jeremy moved his stare to Bacchus' chest. He managed a choking gasp as Bacchus's nipples were swallowed into the flesh of his pectorals and were replaced by tiny mouths of gnashing teeth.

In one swift movement, Bacchus forcefully pushed Jeremy to the bed and flipped him onto his stomach.

Jeremy was able to produce a sudden shriek as the weight of Bacchus came down upon his back. Tears formed in his eyes as the sudden pinpricking of Bacchus' mouthy nipples began chewing upon the skin of his lower shoulder blades as if it was beef jerky. An equivocal agony detonated from head to toe as Jeremy felt the serpent of Bacchus enter his insides. The razor-sharp biting from the anxious mouth of

Bacchus' cock devoured a path into his intestines. When the excruciating agony ignited his viscera, Jeremy's heart ceased.

Should have quit last night was the final thought that incessantly raced through his fretted mind.

Jailed

I knew the terror of it all from the beginning. It was as if all of my fears were balled up into one filthy, crusted rag that was unable to come clean at any cost. Yet, with utmost hesitation, my hopes were optimistic; I wanted to put the entire ordeal behind me.

"What would you do to get out of this place?" The man leaning against the wall had noticed my pacing. At first, I didn't know if he was addressing me or not. But as I turned and retraced my short steps, our eyes made contact beneath the faded white flickering of the overhead lights.

"I can't stand this place. I *need* to get out of here." I directed my complaint to nobody and everybody at the same time. My brain was in frenzy with incessant thoughts and scenarios after three hours. I couldn't imagine being in this place for twenty-four.

Rapid murmurs in a Spanish dialect came from the other corner of the cell. I was sure the Hispanic trio was talking about me in their secret language, probably plotting to kick my ass when "lights out" came, or worse.

"And what would you do to escape this place?" Once again, this coming from the man whose back was against the wall. I wasn't sure if he was making idle conversation or imaginary circumstances to pass the time. After all, time tends to slow for those whose freedom has been stripped.

It feels as if time doesn't exist in jail, as if it is one eternal moment. Each minute is a world of elongated seconds; every sound is but an echo within itself. All of life begins and ends here; this place is the grand Eternal.

My stomach gurgled in hunger because I refused to eat what the guards had passed to the inmates as dinner—warm milk, two pieces of hard bread with a slice of discolored ham, and a soft, wrinkled orange. The odor in the jail cell triggered my stomach into nausea. Although there were ten people in the twenty-four-foot by twelve-foot cell, the body odor that wafted in the air smelled as if I was in a cell of thirty.

A hand caught my shoulder from behind. I swiftly turned, my heart racing and in my throat. The hand belonged to the man who had continuously addressed me. He loomed over me (he was at least five inches taller than I and just as slender).

I reached my hand up to remove his, and he gripped it in a friendly shake. His fingernails practically cut into my wrist. "How long are you in for?" he casually asked. It seemed that was the icebreaker in this place, the language that introduced one as a friend.

I looked him directly in the eyes and suddenly felt calm and scared at the same time. His dark eyes pierced through me and, for one brief moment, I thought that he could see into my mind. "Twenty-four hours," I eagerly spat out.

He laughed toward the ceiling. His smile was perfect, winsome. All his teeth came to perfect points except for the front two that were squared off. In the bad lighting, I saw that his face was smooth and unmarred. The dark goatee that framed his bee-sting lips was perfectly trimmed, matching the shade of his long locks of hair.

"That's all?"

The time I was serving must've been a joke. Of course, it prompted me to ask how long he was to serve. "Yeah, what about you?"

"Oh," he spoke in a delicate baritone voice, "I'm here for a *long* time."

The inmates around us watched our conversation in the center of the cell bloom as if it were a major spectacle.

"What are *you* in for?" I felt silly saying those words. They sounded cliché.

"Theft, among other things," he nonchalantly replied. "How about you?"

"DUI." My eyes fell to the cement floor. I felt ashamed, inferior to this true criminal before me. I quickly changed the subject. "Damn, I need a cigarette," I blurted.

"Come with me," he gestured with a backwards nod.

I followed him a few feet across the cell to his bottom bunk and sat next to him. He leaned over, lifting the thin mattress, and pulled a pack of Marlboro Lights from beneath it. He extracted a cigarette, then a lighter, and handed them to me.

I took a quick glance over to the bars that held me captive. "What about the guards."

He smirked. "They're blind; they won't see a thing."

I lit up the cigarette and experienced an instant, distressing wave rush through me. From the corner of my eye, my new friend watched me suck in the smoke and exhale. "Thanks."

"Not a problem." His replies were so cool, so collected and without worry. "By the way, I'm Alex."

"Sean," I said, taking another eager drag of the cigarette. The other inmates talked amongst themselves and I was no longer the center of attention. There was a great feeling in this; I no longer felt nervous or threatened by, what I perceived as, a group of ruffians.

"So," Alex smoothly said as if he were analyzing me, "are you scared?"

I cocked my head to face him, and I couldn't help but stare at his comely features. If my premature fear of being raped in jail came true, then I prayed that he would be the man doing it. "Should I be scared?"

"What would it take to get you to the other side of those bars?" Our conversation was going nowhere. It seemed to be endless riddles within enigmas.

"A cannon," I laughed. It was the first time I had laughed since I had been jailed.

"Why do you want out so bad?" he asked of me. He interrupted me before I had a chance to respond. "Wait...let's see, you're worried about something." Alex put his hand up as if to halt any gesture of affirmation. "No...some*one*."

I nodded my head and went along with what appeared to be a guessing game.

"A man," Alex remarked, and left it at that.

"Oh god, am I *that* obvious?" Now that my sexuality had been discovered, my feeling of safety burst into the power of threat.

"Don't worry, Sean," Alex consoled, "your secret's safe with me." And he smiled that mischievous but charming smile. Now that he knew I was gay, I tried not to stare at him too long.

I felt a need to explain my situation further and to let it be known to Alex that I wasn't a danger to him. "His name is Derek. We've been together for five years."

"So what are you afraid of?" Alex was suddenly becoming my shrink.

"Well," I paused before admitting, "I've always been the jealous type. Five years is a long time with the same person, especially in the gay culture. I think he's seeing somebody else on the side.

"He knows I'm in here for the night and I know he's going to bring company over to the apartment. I'm going crazy just thinking about it."

"Why don't you just leave him?"

The same thought had crossed my mind many times. There were occasions that our arguments flared to the point of his hitting me. Still, he was my world and I couldn't think to not be by his side. "I love him. He's all I know and want. You can't just leave a person after five years. Besides, I have no proof that he's cheating on me. We had an argument before I left. I have a feeling he's going to leave me. I just want to get out of this place, go back home, and lay next to him."

Alex looked deep into my eyes and grinned. "What's stopping you?"

"Umm, hello, I'm in jail."

"You could be on the other side of those bars if you wanted."

"Yeah right," I offered.

"Just pretend the bars aren't there. What would it take to get you out of this place?"

"You're not serious."

Beyond the bars of the cell, from somewhere down the corridor, a guard yelled, "Lights out."

As the cell went black, there was a momentary lapse of time when Alex's eyes appeared to flicker red.
In the darkness, I felt his hand grab hold of my leg. My body went completely still. "Scared yet?"

-2-

As I lay in bed next to Derek:

> "Sean, you'll be fine. You'll be less stressed once it's done and over with."
> No consoling from him. No contact.
> "Will you miss me?"
> "It will be the first time you haven't been next to me in bed in the five years we've been together. I'm going to be lonely. Of course, I'm going to miss you. I may even be scared in this apartment, all by myself."
> I fell asleep thinking of one word.
> Lonely.

That fear and foreboding endlessly haunted me in the preceding days I was to self-surrender and spend twenty-four hours in the county jail. Of course, I was well aware that I was going to spend a night in jail. I had known since the day I'd plead guilty to the crime of misdemeanor DUI in a "no tolerance" state one month previous. However, hindsight of the fact tended to be blurred a month before that fateful day. Even two weeks before I was to give up a day and night without my freedom, the reality of it all didn't hit me.

Then Monday came, the Monday before the Friday that I was to yield my freedom. That's when the fear began to set in. What was it like to be in such a place? I hadn't a clue; for I had never been in trouble with the law. What type of people would I meet? Disturbing images came to mind, visuals of myself giving a disgruntled inmate a wrong look and having to face incomprehensible actions that would follow.

I abandoned my imaginary scenarios altogether by Monday evening, as I lay in bed next to Derek. He told me it would be all right. But his response seemed auditioned, canned.

He had the perfect opportunity.

The Wednesday before my jail date, I was a wreck. I took the day off work and told my manager I was sick because I couldn't concentrate. My mind was out of focus to the rest of the world, the real world of work, paying bills, and relationships. I only thought of jail, one night in jail. There was no way I could do it! Then again, I had no choice.

I waited all day for Derek to come home. I continuously opened and closed the door to the apartment every time I heard a car coming down the road. However, my actions weren't different from any other day. I always waited by the door for Derek's arrival.

I wondered how his routine would change once I got incarcerated.

Thursday was somewhat of a blur.

I remember waking up as Derek left for work. He always looked so handsome in his business clothes—a Pierre Cardin button down, Perry Ellis slacks, and leather Prada loafers. The colors he wore always matched his features. The color of his dress shirt was often sky blue—it matched his eyes and glorified his gelled, blond locks of hair. And his clothes always fit him with perfection. They hugged his body in a way that his chest appeared dominant and his washboard stomach was obvious beneath his shirt.

I didn't get a kiss before he left, nor did I get a solacing 'I love you.' He went out the door with only a 'goodbye.'

Making another call to work, I explained to my manager that I would not be coming in that day or Friday—I had a flu bug I could not shake. My nerves were so much on edge that my performance on the phone of acting sick was easily executed. My voice trembled as if I had the chills.

Derek didn't call me all morning. *He's drifting away, he doesn't care anymore.*

By noon, I made a quick trip to the neighborhood liquor store where I purchased a bottle of Jack Daniels. Good old Jack, he always listened to me and consoled me with his liquor tongue.

I drank shot after shot of my fluidic redeemer, and the world felt better. Beneath the veil of alcohol that consumed my body, there was no jail date, no crime ever committed by me, and it felt as if I were on a vacation from work. Everything was fine save for my feelings of Derek's alleged infidelity. I had to keep him! When exactly did he fail to notice me? What was it that caused him to despise me? Was it the fact that I was now considered a "criminal?" No, it wasn't that at all. It was my jealousy and he had told me this on a number of occasions.

Yet, the jealousy wasn't always there. Something triggered it, some anti-trust on his part. And there was the feeling, that awful gut instinct that we're always told to follow. That sensation had run rampant through me for the past six months. *He's with somebody else. He doesn't love you anymore. You're kidding yourself living this way. Let him go.*

But he's all I know.

I walked to the mirror and gazed at myself, taking quick notice of my bloodshot eyes and the tired expression upon my face. My brown hair had seemed to lose its shine and had grown longer than I would've ever allowed it to. The face in the mirror was haggard. Premature lines were prominent around my mouth and at the edges of my eyes. The luminescence of my green eyes was veritably extinguished. I had lost weight. What was I becoming?

Throughout the day, my jealous thoughts brimmed. By the time Derek got home, they came out full force.

We got into an argument, but I don't remember the vicious words. In fact, I only remember yelling. There were unintelligible curses flung in every direction around us.

The entire confrontation is still nothing but a black void in my mind to this day.

-3-

    I trembled in the darkness. Part of it had to do with the freezing temperature in the cell. A shivering breath rushed over my lips as I attempted to ignore Alex's hand on my leg.

    "What do you want?" I shuddered at the thought of his answer.

    "I want to know if you're scared." He spoke in a normal tone, instead of a whisper in the darkness.

    "Do you want me to be scared?"

    "I want to do whatever I can to get you to the other side of those bars so that you can face your fear."

    "My fear?"

    "Yes, Sean, your fear of what Derek is doing right now while you're trapped in here. You need to face your fear. You know, in your heart, what Derek has done. You know exactly what he is doing right now as we speak."

    "I have no proof."

    "But the proof is beyond the bars of this cell, I assure you."

    I decided to play along with Alex's delusion. "OK, let's say I could get to the other side of those bars. Why does my personal life matter to you?"

    There was a brief pause, and then, "I suppose there is something in it for me."

    "Ah. You see; I knew you wanted something."

    "All I would ask is that you do the same in return for me."

    "I don't understand."

    "If I could give you your freedom, I would ask that you give me mine as well."

    "OK," I gave off a slight chuckle. "You break me out of this place and I'll come back for you. There. OK, make the bars disappear now." I followed my remark of sarcasm with, "yeah right."

    Alex let out an exasperated breath as if he were frustrated. "Do you want to go through your life being trapped by your unconfirmed thoughts of what Derek is getting away with?"

    I shook my head without saying a word. I felt my heart race a bit more as the conversation ensued, as Alex confirmed my hidden feelings.

    The entire setting with Alex in the darkness, two convicts sitting in a murky jail cell, ignited the giddiness of a dream. And there was a part of me somewhere, beyond my raging thoughts of jealousy, that begged to believe this was a dream. Alex couldn't be serious. What was I to do, simply walk out of jail and past the guards? It was ridiculous and I was reluctant to entertain the thought any longer. "Perhaps we should just go to sleep," I offered.

"I can get you to the other side of those bars," Alex continued with his impossible plan to free me.

"I'm going to sleep."

I went to stand up from his bunk and go to my own, but his hand tightened on my leg, causing me to remain seated next to him. "Leave me alone, or I'm calling for the guards," I raised my voice.

I felt the hand on my leg release and I quickly made my way to the other side of the cell. Alex called from behind me. "Don't forget, you promised to come back for me."

"Whatever," I mumbled.

"Sean," Alex said. "Are you ready to be scared?"

I froze from the delicate whisper of his words that came from behind and wrapped around my galloping heart. I was mesmerized by the power of that question, as if such a pending threat could sound so seductive at the same time.

With my body turned away from Alex, a trickle of heat washed my back like beads of sweat rushing down my flesh. Suddenly, the darkness of the cell became illuminated. It began with an orange flickering, like that of a wild candle that illuminated a patch of the cemented wall before me. The glowing crept along the wall and spread out in all directions. That's when I noticed the elongated features of my shadow. The light came from behind, from the direction where Alex sat. I remained stock-still, hypnotized by the source of the illumination and fearing what possible scene could be taking place from where I had my back turned.

In my peripheral vision, I scanned the other inmates who were fast asleep and unaware of the phenomena engulfing the cell. I had to turn around, had to face the source of this wicked creation. But, at the same time, my stomach crawled and folded as I trembled in my steps.

My fears were confirmed when I heard what could only be described as a static buzzing that played in symphony with a crackling of dead leaves. My blood raced through my veins, my adrenaline shocking my heart and brain. And in those moments, the terrifying moments of fear unknown—a world infiltrated by buzzing and crackling and an impossible glowing—Alex's words echoed in my mind. *Are you ready to be scared?*

I anticipated turning around until I heard his voice again. "Sean," he called. But his tone was different. His inflection was deep and vibrated off the walls of the cell. I practically fell in my rapid pivot as I confronted

Alex; for I wasn't prepared for the horrifying being that had stood in Alex's place.

Behind the looming figure, and orange ball of brilliance ignited its features into view. It was as if flames danced all about its visage and form, revealing the metamorphoses of Alex into the horrific creature that came into view. The cinnamon skin tone that had once belonged to Alex had grown maroon in color. Its earlier smooth texture was now shriveled and appeared rough, like some fleshy armor. From its robust chest down to its bulging calves, its muscles pulsed in accord to the cadence of my own heart. From its narrow fingers and toes, elongated blue-black nails ejected. Its harrowing face comprised sunken eyes with colorless irises, no nose save for two triangular slits embedded flat upon its face, and a long, sharp smile that bore rows of uneven and jagged teeth that came to piercing tips. The creature's head was absent of hair. All that remained upon its wrinkled and bloodied scalp were three lumps (two an inch higher then the third in between).

The orange illumination behind it flared, pulsed, and grew brighter. I was aghast by the creature, lost in a realm that teetered between reality and mythological monsters. My body involuntarily backed itself as far as it could, until I felt the top bunk behind me press hard against my shoulders.

It spoke. It spoke the way demons do in Hollywood, with a snarl and an echoing resonance so unreal it could only come from such a monster. "Does this scare you, Sean?" Its triple-forked tongue slid across its upper lip in appetite.

I made a quick glance at the other inmates who remained asleep to the ghastly form that inhabited the cell. Above their slumbering bodies, transparent clouds of blue and red colors tied into ghostly knots and weaved into themselves. Why didn't they wake from the luminescence or by the timbering voice of the monster that shared the cell with them?

This isn't real! This is a dream! I made a panicked affirmation. *Derek, I need you here! Yes, a dream. I'm dreaming and Derek is going to wake me up and tell me that my mind is stressed from the thought of going to jail.*

As if the creature had read my mind, it confirmed otherwise. "This is no dream, Sean. This is real." The creature reached to me with outstretched arms and brought its five digits of each hand together. Its nails clicked together as one. It did this repeatedly. *Click, dick, dick.* The clicking continued and the beat was that of a second hand that rounded the face of a clock. *Click, dick, dick (tic, tic, tic). Time running out.*

"What do you want?" My voice attacked the creature.

"I'm going to eat you, Sean. I'm going to savor your flesh and consume your soul."

The adrenaline speeding throughout my body put my heart into overdrive. I ran to the cell door and tightly grabbed the bars as I screamed, "Guards! Guards! Oh God, help me!"

The cell grew brighter in orange light. I turned to see the creature approaching me. *Click, click, click,* its nails continued as it reached out to me. Its mouth opened impossibly wide. Its upper jaw folded completely backward, parallel to the lower half of its jowl, to reveal hundreds of jagged teeth. Its tongue ejected from the center like a fleshy fountain reaching for the ceiling of the cell.

I screeched a siren tone I had never heard come from my vocal chords before. Hastily, I pushed the cell door back and forth. The iron lock clanged a melody of fear and fortitude.

As I turned again, the creature was two feet behind me. *Click, click, click.* Its tongue wavered in the air. I feared it would come down on me and wrap around my body as it pulled me into the mouth of the creature. I pushed my entire weight against the cell door, pushing and pulling, as my body became one with the cold, iron bars.

The door swung open and I fell to the floor beyond the cell. I refused to turn back to observe the creature's distance from me. With apprehension as my driving catalyst, I scampered to my feet and began sprinting down the corridor.

There were no guards, not a single person in sight, to witness my escape.

As I got further down the hall, I noticed the emergency exit directly before me. As I reached it, I used all of my strength to push it wide open without halting my run. I ejected from the county jail with the velocity of a bullet exiting the barrel of a gun.

Within the eerily quiet parking lot, I found my car in no time. As the engine revved, I observed the entire building of the county jail grow bright as the sun.

I was going home and the nightmare was now behind me.

-4-

I gasp for breath.
Blue. Everything is blue, like swimming in a magnificent and endless sea. Like freefalling, zero gravity. Blue. The blues. I've got the blues and I've got a bottle of Jack in my hand. Nothing better to take the blues away.

The sea is so cold, so empty. Empty save for the fish. Fish—their scaly textures brushing against my body, near my face, and against my throat.
I need to go up for air. Don't want to be blue forever, no.
Lonely.

-5-

The door was unlocked as I rushed into the apartment. This late at night, and I can't believe how many times I had told Derek about locking the door.

"Derek," I called out. All the lights in the place were extinguished except for the lamp in the hallway. *Perhaps he's sleeping.* It didn't matter. I needed him to wake up. And I didn't care of the consequences of my escape from that horrible place. That is, if the building was there any longer. In fact, I would probably be known as the only survivor of the night when some freak of nature accident took down and killed all who inhabited the county jail.

"Derek," I yelled for him again. I locked the door behind me. I could hear a grunting sound emerge from down the hallway. Not one grunt, but two.

My mind instantly created the scenario that went with those grunts. I quickly realized I didn't want to see what I feared. But I knew I had to confront it. No fiber of my being wanted it to be true, but I still had to know. I had to have the proof I sought; I had to confirm my fears. Just like Alex had told me. Alex, a man turned monster.

I slowly progressed down the length of the hallway, each step into the plush carpet silent and uncertain. To the right of me was the guest bedroom and to the left was the bedroom of which Derek and I had shared for the past five years. Our bedroom door was cracked open and I could see the shadowy outlines of two bodies upon the bed.

I wept within myself. My head throbbed in agony, in a pain that broken love can only create. I gently pushed the door open and the light of the hallway spilt into the room, revealing the heartbreak that awaited me.

There lay Derek, his blond hair tussled, beneath the weight of another man who thrust into him. Their bodies moved in a lustful, sexual wave that ours used to. The stranger behind Derek draped his hands over Derek's shoulders, feeling Derek's chest as he repeatedly forced his hips into Derek. They groaned together in a sexual murmur shared in the act of such lovemaking.

Tears welled in my eyes, blurring the scene. The heated droplets rushed down my face. "Derek," a broken plea came from my voice. "Why did you do this to us?"

Derek cocked his head toward where I stood. His piercing eyes went through me and he smiled in ecstasy from his lover's actions. No words came from him, no shock at discovering that I had caught him in the act.

I wanted to scream. In fact, I wanted to run to the bed and jump on the two of them with flailing fists and scolding words. But he didn't care for me and I hadn't the energy to change my destiny.

Drifting from the frame of the doorway, I walked into the guest bedroom. I shut the door behind me and sat upon the edge of the bed. My tears ran full force now. All I could think of was that I was right all along. Alex was right. Perhaps the creature Alex had morphed into was saving me. Perhaps.

The bed I sat upon was unmade. I found it rather strange as Derek and I never used this bed. Looking behind me, I noticed another body in the bed. They were covered, asleep. It was hard enough to comprehend Derek's infidelity, but it appeared that the man he was in bed with right now was but one of two, if not many. *That bastard*, I mentally scolded.

I was sick of being scared, tired of being the victim. It was time to stand up and stop this emotional charade. First, I would take care of this one, right there in the same bed upon which I sat. Then, I would traipse into the other bedroom—MY bedroom—and tell Derek and his new beau to leave. Yes, I was going to kick Derek out of the apartment, out of my life, and start all over again.

I reached over to pull the sheet back from the sleeping enemy. A jolt of energy burst into my heart as I forced myself to blink twice. I repeated to myself that this was all one bad nightmare—the creature in the cell, Derek's infidelity, and now this.

What lay before me, motionless and with eyes wide open was a reflection of myself. I lay there naked. My eyes were clouded over; my flesh was faintly blue. Around my neck, I observed the swollen purple imprints made by hands. I screeched in horror, but no sound emerged from my throat.

In brisk flashes, the black, drunken void of Thursday became clear. The confrontation between Derek and me, my jealousy emerging, his hands choking the life from my shell—all of those images passed quickly though my mind.

With that realization, I began to hear a familiar, harrowing sound.

Click, click, click.

It was Alex, the monster with whom I had struck a deal. Yes, I promised I would come back for him in return for my freedom.

The room around me swirled and twisted into a funnel turned on its side. At the very end of it, I could see the creature's mouth wide-open, waiting for me to come back. I felt my body, ever so weightless, drifting beyond the swirls that blended into abstract pictures of what had once been my reality and toward Alex's hungry mouth.

I knew the terror of it all from the beginning. But, perhaps, I wanted to deny the awful truth. Now, the clicking nails of the creature that awaits me, is like that of a gavel coming down repeatedly.

As I floated toward its mouth, I shuddered at the thought of what my sentence would be.

If Not For Death

Fragile, like a baby in his arms. The skin of the young man is soft and delicate, and his tender flesh gives off a faint smell of talc, like that of a newborn: fresh and innocent. His hair has a subtle ginger tint that runs through the silky strands. Jaded eyes are wide open, expressionless and not giving off a glimmer of life, save for a glistening due to a hint of tears wantering from death's embrace. The boy could be no older than nineteen, but his naked body is built like a healthy man that has dedicated hours to lifting weights and hardening his body. His pectorals are exquisite semi-orbs that create a deep, hairless groove in between them; his, now limp, cock is longer than the man had ever seen (definitely not that of a boy); and the young man's angelic face is clean-shaven with succulent lips pressed together. No grin except the reddened gash of a smile that runs from one double-pierced ear to the other.

James Grant held the lifeless corpse, gripping it tightly in his arms. He interlaced his fingers together as his forearms embraced either side of the young man's head. James' hands rested upon the kid's chest, the kid who called himself Geoff when he was alive. The bloody streams that ran from the laceration along Geoff's throat were beginning to dry, crust, and flake from around the area that James' hands rested.

He held on to Geoff for more than three hours now, never wanting to let the boy go. He was his newest love, the newest piece of art that James' would soon add to his collection (frozen, abstract love). Besides, nobody would miss Geoff, for only James' loved the young man and not anybody else. Nobody missed the others, after all. The other three were a love unbridled that were preserved in James' maddening mind just as they had been embedded in the guest bedroom wall. That was where he normally made love to them, in the guest bedroom. However, he felt closer to this one. This one, he would have in his own bed because James' feelings for this one were stronger than that of the others. It seemed that his love for them grew stronger each time.

Promises, he knew each and every one. They each promised everything in the world when he touched the knife to their inviting throats from behind. They always begged before death came. James remembered one, probably the second (he thought his name was Dave or Dale), that said he would live with him forever and succumb to James' every wish. James took the fretted kid up on his offer, deeply slashing the boy's throat, and the whiner did indeed stay with James to this date.

Their pledges were no different from that of Kyle's. Kyle promised to love James, honor him, and always be faithful. *Lying prick*, James angrily thought as he recollected his love a year and a half previous. The point at which James had snapped was after Kyle left with that ugly looking, drag queen bitch. After that, anything James loved would become his until the end of time. And there was no stopping him.

In the evening hours, James nonchalantly slithered his way through the maze of skyscrapers beneath the polluted atmosphere of Phoenix. Two miles north was Central Avenue, the heart of Gay Phoenix. It was this heart that contained all his loves upon its sidewalks. There was always lots of activity on Central: from the filthy male hustlers that gave blowjobs in bum-infested alleys for a twenty spot, to gay gentlemen hitting the various clubs along the strip, and even, ironically, Phoenix's own protecting and serving police department. They never had a clue as to what happened to any of the men James had abducted. The boys became mere faces reported missing and ended up on postcard mailers.

Stravinsky's *Rites of Spring* methodically blared throughout the confines of James' apartment. Classical music was the best. It was so cunning, mysterious and subtle. Then came the climax, like a killer lunging for his helpless victim. *Helpless*. James could use his charm to lure any of the boys to his place. He knew the way to talk; he was aware of what they wanted to hear. He hadn't met a young, gay male in the area yet that hadn't succumbed to the politics of romanticism. Give them attention and give them a lot; make them feel like they are the most exquisite creatures upon which eyes had ever cast; and, then, preserve that love they have for you. This thrilled James more than anything did. It was better than any moment when he orgasmed inside a young man's virgin ass. It was more of a rush than tasting the smooth milky texture of his victims before they died. Yes, he could make anybody love him. Anybody. He was the puppet master of all his boys' emotions, the eternal god of love they would have no choice but to worship. He would be their Adonis.

He observed the corpse he clung to as the classical CD ended. The body had grown cold and it stared blankly up to James. He stroked the young man's hair (Geoff, wasn't it?). "Dear, dear, Geoff. I love you too," he said to the boy. Unfortunately, James realized, Geoff was unable to move about. His body was expired and his love for James had deadened. Gone, but not forgotten. No. It was time to place him behind the wall, along with his other human dolls.

After he would place the man that called himself Geoff behind a secret wall that held the morbid collage of his partners, it would be time, once again, to traipse through the city streets in search of a new love. Geoff was victim number four and number five was only an hour or so away. James used to be able to go a couple of days before seizing another, but this obsessive search for his loves became an addiction. The young men were his needles and he was in need of a fix. Badly in need.

Forty-five minutes later, James had managed to store Geoff's body—kissing him gently on the boy's frigid, bluish lips—clean the bed by disposing the bloodstained sheets, and showered. Upon turning off the lights and leaving the apartment, he heard *it*. *It* sounded like a quick gasp of breath followed by a subtle exhale. It was almost like an exasperated cry of a child timed to the brisk rhythm of a heartbeat. *Thump-thump. Thud-thud. Quick-breath. Huh-huh.*

"SHUT UP," James hollered. The resonance of his voice wildly bounced off the apartment walls. He locked his hands tightly against his ears, not allowing a single sound into his eardrums save for the muffled quickening of his own heartbeat. The sound stopped. *It* always went away when he did that.

***

"I don't want to die," the young man mumbled in tones of sorrow, possibly apologizing to any god who might be listening. If there was any entity "upstairs", he only prayed that it heard his plea. *The only time; that one time.* It wasn't as if he were as promiscuous as all those guys at the club. Those guys, he envisioned, in their tight jeans and their faggy gestures that came on to anything and everything as long as it was a good fuck.

Cole Stevens anticipated down Central's sidewalks. He walked past johns who offered him a good time and didn't bother to acknowledge them, let alone look up from the sidewalk that his DC's had trod so far upon. It must have been six miles now, from the prostitute-infested Van Buren Street to Camelback Road.

The only way Cole knew how to deal with his present crisis was by walking. He had always preferred jumping behind the wheel of his Maxima versus the exercising of his legs. Tonight, however, he desperately needed to take his mind off this undying cancer that ate at both his brain and body. He replayed the terrifying scenes of his life, the life that had gulped down the last seven of his years in worry and insecurity.

When Cole was seventeen, he...(yes, he remembered that party). That was the particular party that he didn't bring a condom with him.

The party where he got drunk and came on to that ravishing twenty-two year old that he knew had been around the block in more ways than one. That was the same party that began his new life of living in fear. Since that night, the thought of HIV had revisited him, from his haunting dreams to his imaginary symptoms. And through that interim of his life, worry and hypochondria had become his new best friends. Every little spot, each time he broke out in an inexplicable sweat, and every day that he had become weak, Cole wrestled with the thought of having the virus. Of course, he could have ended the mental torment and gone for a test, but that was a giant leap. He would rather not know if he had a death sentence. Some days he felt fine, other days he was convinced he had contracted the virus. This morning, however, when he peered at his chest in the mirror and saw those three deep, purplish lesions, he had a definite answer. And now, he had no choice but to cope with it.

Up to this morning, Cole trusted that the idea of having HIV was just a byproduct of his own fears. Not any more. He had it. And, after seeing those dreaded symptoms in the mirror, his body shot into a state of panic. His heart raced, hot flashes attacked him from all sides, and he called off work. He paced around his apartment before he began traipsing the path of the local hustlers and drag queens.

What was he to do? Indeed, this was the end of the world! He had so much life to live and so many dreams he wanted to accomplish. How could he tell his friends? His family? More horrible than that, how many people had he infected with the virus? There were casual lovers that were long out of his life, true loves that he swore he would never leave and eventually got over. Now what was he supposed to do? Bring them back into his life to tell them that he had unknowingly infected them with a virus?

Central Avenue was busy. Cars drove past Cole, some honking horns and others with passengers that whistled at him and asked 'how much?' Hell, he thought, he might as well have been a hustler. After all, he had the virus that went with the territory. The scary thing was that these innocent people driving in their cars had no clue of the night he could give them, a night that would affect their lives more than they could imagine. Even scarier was the thought that none of them probably cared. People never tend to care about such things until it physically impairs their lives and makes its horrific mark.

"I don't want to die," Cole continued mumbling to himself. "Please, God, don't let it be true." Unfortunately, he knew it was true. This was his new life, and he had no choice but to live with it until Death reached out its inviting arms and embraced him with its anticipated touch.

A later model Mitsubishi Eclipse pulled alongside the road in front of Cole. The passenger side window rolled down and the driver casually shouted a "Hi."

"Sorry, man," Cole responded, "I'm not a hustler."

The man inside the sports car was older, probably in his early thirties. He was a handsome and intelligent looking man with wavy, shoulder-length blond hair and thin coke-bottle spectacles that framed his intriguing eyes.

"You all right?" the man in the car asked worriedly. *Yes*, the man thought, this exquisite young man was definitely his new love. Oh, the pleasures he could have with this one. His short-cropped, black hair painted over such a ravishing face that bled hints of Italian blood. Smooth almond skin that could melt fingertips. Fragile skin. Baby's flesh.

Cole was muddled by the stranger's question. Why would the man care? Yet, his other friends weren't around. It happened that way in these days; friends were friends until you needed them to hold you and tell you things would be fine (even though they were not). When you needed those friends in times like these, watch out; for that is when you realize that the only person you have to depend on is yourself. And when you're already weak and dying and can barely hold it all together, that is when you've reached your lowest point. Indeed, this was Cole's low point in life.

He was speechless to the man's question. He didn't know how to respond. Should he confide his disease-infested thoughts to the stranger or should he pretend it was all in his head and enjoy the company of another person? Cole made his decision in the spur of the moment, and the latter felt like the better of the two.

He opened the passenger side door and ducked into the company of the stranger's vehicle, forgetting, if only for tonight, the harsh reality of mortal life.

The stranger smiled as Cole offered his hand and introduced himself.

"I'm James," the stranger announced. "Want to head back to my place?"

Although Cole knew it was a bad idea, and it had gone against everything he had ever believed about one-night-stands, he shook his head yes.

James revved the Eclipse's engine and threw the car into first gear, second, and third in a matter of moments. How he longed to take Cole to his home, into his arms and taste that delicate flesh, feel that golden body upon his own, and preserve his love in a memorabilia of madness.

***

Upon reaching the apartment, after passing a deliciously inviting, gated swimming pool and climbing a flight of zigzag stairs, Cole watched as James unlocked the Schlage deadbolt on the door. There was a similar lock below it. Finally, Cole observed the man insert another key into the slit in the door handle itself, before it eased opened.

What's this guy so paranoid about? Cole curiously wondered. Curious. Wonder. The wonders of how poisoned his insides were plagued Cole's frightened mind. He looked to his smooth forearms and observed his flesh constricting around puffed veins. Somewhere in those veins traveled a silent killer. With that horrible idea at hand, Cole instantly tried dismissing it. No, he couldn't die so young in life. *Forget it. Don't think about it.*

"Come on in, Cole," James gestured with his hand toward the entryway.

As Cole sauntered in, he was instantly astounded by the cleanliness of the place. The armchair and couch appeared to be brand new, a soft beige color that was tough to keep stains from showing. A small bookshelf lined the wall opposing the front door. All the books were hard-covered; their spines came to the edge of the shelf in an even line. The entertainment system was enormous—a fifty-two inch high-definition television, Sony Blu-Ray and compact disc player. The audio CD's were separate from the digital, stored in a small, black rotunda organizer and alphabetized by artist name.

The apartment smelled of bleach, Pine-Sol, Pledge, or maybe all three. The tan, plush carpet lacked any kind of debris and appeared new, as if it had been recently steam-cleaned. Maybe that was the clean smell that wafted throughout the room. Christ, even the foot traffic area in the path of the doorway lacked any sign of matted carpet.

James closed the door behind Cole, locked the knob, and twisted the two locks above it. Although this slightly set unease within Cole, he dismissed it. After all, he had worse things to worry about.

"A glass of wine?" the host asked.

"Sure." Yeah, wine. That would keep his mind off things, for tonight anyway. "Red wine."

James gave off a cockish laugh that seemed fake and absent of true emotion. "But, of course. Have a seat. I'll be back in a sec." Upon his departure from the room James commented, "You know, they say red wine builds the blood."

Blood, Cole thought. *Blood-building. Poison strengthened.*

He sat upon the Lazyboy rocker and threw his right leg over his left. Cole studied the room as he heard the subtle clanking of wine glasses emerge from the kitchen. A gigantic gold-framed print of Van Gogh's *Starry Night* was centered on the opposing wall, and he couldn't help but wonder if the gold was real. His gaze traced the swirls of the picture and he could only imagine himself lost in that world of peaceful darkness, a world of tranquil night and beautiful, beaming stars bathing his body in warmth and comfort.

James re-entered the room with two glasses of wine and handed one to Cole. From the looks of the deep redness, it could only be merlot or cabernet. He grasped the glass and, before he raised it to his lips, his host interjected.

James raised his glass to Cole's. "To new friends," he cheered. Their glasses slightly brushed together and emitted a muffled *dink*.

The taste of the merlot passed Cole's lips and swathed his tongue in a warm, tangy bitterness. It raced down his throat and swarmed in his stomach. Ahhhhh, a couple more of these is what he needed.

"You have a nice place," Cole complimented.

"Yeah? The bedroom's this way." James began to make small steps toward the bedroom while keeping his eyes on Cole.

Cole hesitated, remaining seated. He knew what James wanted. After all, you just don't pick up somebody you've never met, bring them home, and cater drinks to them for no reason. Would he be able to do this? *Could* he do this? He didn't even have a condom on him. Shouldn't he break the news about his affliction to his anxious host?

James waited and pondered if the exquisite boy was going to follow him to the bedroom. Or would he try running for the door, saying he made a mistake and that this wasn't what he wanted? It wouldn't work, the madman cleverly reminded himself. He would reach the boy before Cole knew what hit him. James would use force if he had to. It wouldn't be the first time.

Quick breath.

Without warning, the enigmatic and annoying sound flooded James' head. *Thump-thump.* It blared, filling his ears and pulsing in his thoughts.

Huh-huh.....quick breath.....huh-huh.

"Stop," James casually commanded, afraid that Cole would hear him in this mysterious state.

"What?"

"Nothing, Cole. I have to use the bathroom. I'll meet you in the bedroom, O.K.?"

Cole nodded in reply as James hurried to the bathroom. He wondered if the guy was going to get sick off one glass of wine. "What the hell," he said to himself as he rose and headed toward the bedroom.

When he reached it and flipped on the light switch, he found a very simple bedroom—a single bed and a tiny, four-drawer dresser made of oak or cherry wood. Nothing too far out of the ordinary; however, nothing on the walls either. Blank. There was no character to the room. It looked like a cheap motel one would check into for the night. Also, the smell in here was slightly different. The aroma of cleaning liquids faintly filled the air, but there was also another smell that blended in with it. A pungent smell, the smell of rotting meat   He sat at the edge of the bed and waited for his host to return.

***

Huh-huh. Huh-huh. Huh-huh. Quick breath.

What originally started as a faint whispering now blared through James' head like the clamorous sounds of a percussionist pounding upon a timpani tuned to C-Flat.

"Stop," he called aloud to the invisible assassins of vibration.
Huh-huh. Huh-huh. Huh-huh.

It thundered in his head, a storm of quick breaths like that of a dying person. Louder and louder, *it* trumpeted. *It* filled his mind, invaded his own breathing, and made synchronism with his heartbeat. Pulsing, thumping, breathing, overwhelming his being and his will until James could take no more.

"STOP IT, "he commanded as he reached for his ears. Then he hammered his reflection in the mirror with a flat slap onto the silvery glass.

Gone. *It* was gone again. James realized that this time *it* put up more of a fight than ever. Then another thought eclipsed that one altogether. The thought of his new love, Cole. He was the one, indeed! How he had grown to love this exquisite youth. He *had* to have him.

***

Cole promptly stood to his feet. What in the hell was going on in the bathroom? Was there somebody else in the apartment? In the bathroom with James?

That thought still at hand, James barreled around the corner and into the bedroom. Cole immediately recoiled as James raised his scornful voice. "What are you doing in *here*?"

"What?" Cole questioned. *Didn't he say to 'meet him in the bedroom?* The look in the man's eyes was that of fury, as if he were ready to pounce upon Cole and rip him to shreds.

"I'm sorry," James instantly apologized. "This is the guest room. My room is the other one across from here. Please, come with me."

Cole walked passed the troubled man and into the other bedroom. It was at this time, at the time he prodded alongside his strange host, that he began to feel extremely uncomfortable.

This bedroom, James' bedroom, was not much different from the guest room, save for the nineteen-inch Sony television and traditional DVD player. As with the guest room, the walls in the room were blank. This struck Cole as odd. After all, people usually adorn their bedrooms with some signature of themselves, whether it pictures, posters of their favorite artists, or even cheap-framed, superstore lithographs.

He sat upon the edge of the bed and the flowery aroma of Bounce fabric softener filled his nostrils. Once again, here he sat, at the edge of some stranger's bed, waiting for the man to enter. Suddenly, the relaxing sounds of classical music invaded the awkward silence.

James set foot into the room with a bottle of Merlot in his hand. He eased himself upon the bed beside Cole. "Hope you don't mind the music."

"Not at all," Cole replied.

After three more glasses of wine and an hour and a half of intense conversation, Cole felt more comfortable with the man who had invited him to his apartment. Their discussion mainly consisted of classical musicians, which was an awesome subject to Cole as he always enjoyed falling to sleep to the sounds of Beethoven and Chopin. This type of music relaxed him, made him forget all the troubles of the day, just as it did now. At that point, his mind lingered further than it had the entire day from the thought of the virus. In fact, his thoughts were in a haze from all the wine that he had taken into his system. Not to mention, he hadn't eaten all day due to his stress-induced state.

"Yes," James stated, "Chopin is a master at his art."

He watched as Cole smiled in agreement. That luscious smile that he wanted his lips to touch and his body to become one with in heated passion. He felt the emotion of love (a murderer's lust) come about. In that perfect moment, he reached out his hand and placed it beneath Cole's smooth chin.

Cole trembled. However, he projected his mind past his nervousness and penetrated James' intently staring eyes with his own.

James gently tugged on the young man's chin, pulling his face close to his own, and fervently planted his lips upon his newfound lover's mouth. Their tongues tangled in a dance of horniness. James slid his hand upon Cole's jeans, from his knee to his inner thigh, toward his crotch. He was getting excited, wanted to take this young man and savagely rip through his clothing, pulverizing him until he was nothing but a limp body in his arms. Yes, Cole was the one James could love forever. He would stay with James throughout all of eternity. The *feeling* informed James of this. Yes, *that* feeling, that tingling sensation that ran throughout his body, grazing the ends of his nerves and making him feel forever loved.

Cole felt the man's hand massaging his cock and instantly got a hard-on. He continued kissing, swapping his bile fluids with this man and penetrating James mouth. Morbidly, Cole mentally questioned how long it would be before he developed thrush. James unzipped Cole's CK jeans and pulled out his throbbing cock, briskly attacking it with his mouth and slobbering all about it. Cole only wondered if the poison of HIV in his semen would shoot down this man's throat and infect his body seven to ten years from now. As James moved his hand up under Cole's t-shirt, kneading the young man's hardened chest, Cole recoiled altogether. He pulled his cock from James mouth and placed the rock-hard organ back into his pants. He leapt off the bed. The ashamed horror of James feeling the KS lesions, or even seeing them, threw Cole into shock. He couldn't do this! No, not to an innocent person. Not without saying something. Cole may have felt the beginnings of a drunken stupor, but he wasn't that dumb.

"All right," James responded in frustration, "what's the problem?"

Cole tucked his shirt into his jeans. "I'm sorry, James. I can't do this. I mean, you're a great guy and all but...I just can't."

What? What was this? He *can't*? Was Cole saying he didn't love him? Because James loved Cole and Cole *had* to love James. Was the young man going to leave? If that was the case, James was already mentally planning how he would stop Cole before exiting the bedroom. The straight-razor was right beneath the pillow. James would have him, nonetheless. It wouldn't be his first experience of necrophilia. "Was it something I did?" James voice took on a different tone, more high-pitched and defensive.

Huh-huh.....huh-huh. It started very silently, like a minute hum that was beginning and then slowly dissipating..

"No; it's not you. It's me."

No, James thought, *he can't leave. He is my love. My true love. Huh-huh.....quick breath.....ha-ha.* Stop it, his mind ordered. *Hush.*

That's it, hush. Think, James, think.

"That's fine then," James casually responded. "I understand. But can I at least ask you to lie down with me and let me hold you?"

Cole's mind slowly reached a point of contentment. It was rather sad. Finally, a man that cared, a man that didn't need sex but just wanted to hold on to somebody. And that's what Cole needed more than anything: some caring soul to hold him. He only wished that he didn't have this godawful virus; for he surely knew he could be in a long term relationship with James. Unfortunately, reality reared its ugly head. They called it Murphy's Law.

"That would be fine," Cole agreed. "I would like that a lot."

It was the finest music to James' ears, like the diminishing sounds of Beethoven's *Eroica*. It was the night's fantasy come true, an act that would lead into the art of preservation.

James sat up at the head of the bed, his back against the down pillows. He spread his legs wide, so that Cole could sit between them and rest his head upon his chest. Then, James would wrap his arms around the man he'd instantly grown to love and hold him close to his body. Two physical beings becoming one entity of love.

He watched as Cole climbed upon the bed, like a mischievous panther, and fell back against James warm and inviting body. James wrapped his arms around him and hugged him tightly like an oversized teddy bear.

Cole writhed in the attention. He shut his eyes and rested; he fell into the reverie of drunkenness that seduced his body just as James had. The wonderful effects of a good wine made his body numb, slightly tingly, and submissive. This was exactly what he sought since first discovering the dreaded site upon his chest that morning. Solace.

Huh-huh.....huh-huh. The psychotic man that held his forever love heard *it* begin again. He didn't want to hear *it* and, instead, poured all of his focus upon the man he held. James stroked the young man's flinty hair that contained gel, or mousse, or hairspray—vital products in a world of beauty and sadness.

Oh, how Cole felt the comfort that stormed about his chest and head. The consoling touches and grazes of James' fingers made him feel relieved and wanted, even though a virus writhed within him.

Huh-huh.....huh-huh.....huh-huh.....ha-ha.....ha-ha. The annoying and driven phantom sounds emerged louder throughout James' being. At first, like those never forgotten, dying breaths; then, like the sounds of insidious laughter. He tried willing them away with mental yelling and realized they would not go. For some reason, they were here to stay this time. Each quick breath grew louder and got closer.

"I love you, Cole." James spoke, trying to make the sounds vanish with his audio confession.

Love? Cole was suddenly confused. He had just met James. How could he love him?

Huh-huh.....ha-ha.....HUH-HUH.....HA-HA!

"I LOVE YOU," he voiced again. James endeavored at making his point strident, in an attempt to eclipse the noisier sounds that drowned his mind.

HUH-HUH.....HA-HA!

Still no reply from Cole, and James began to experience an empty sense of abandonment. As if he and Cole had been a long term item and the man no longer loved him. Just like Kyle had done. But he would *make* Cole love.

HUH-HUH.....HA-HA.....HA-HA!

Cole lay silent, eyes fluttering in contemplation of the words to say.

James took his right hand, the hand with which he had stroked fingers through Cole's hair, and reached beneath the pillow for the straight razor. In all slyness, he pulled it out, opened it, and placed the blade against the tender flesh of Cole's throat.

Cold. The young man's word search ended as he felt the iciness of something sharp prick his throat. Then, a tinge of a slice; enough to feel a slight burn, enough to know blood had been drawn.

More than ever, Cole lay utterly frozen. He only spoke, "What are you doing, James?" He couldn't fathom James taking this sort of action, and the realization of it all launched him into an astonished terror.

"I-"

HUH-HUH.....HUH-HUH.....

"said I"

HUH-HUH.....HUH-HUH.....HA-HA.....

"love YOU!" James hollered, gripping tightly at the razor's handle and applying more pressure against delicate skin.

HA-HA.....HA-HA.....HA-HA.....

"Please," Cole pleaded for his life, knowing that he could not move. It would only take one swipe of the razor before his neck could be sliced from ear to ear. The adrenaline burst and terror enveloped his body, as he not only was threatened by death from the inside of his body, but now from the outside as well.

"I love you, Cole," James made his final declaration. It was time. Time to preserve Cole's love and then seize his body and make him his forever.

The horrid sounds grew magnificently uproarious and surged through James mind. Breath. Laughter. Close and closer and closest.

Suddenly, before James could make his signature incision to mark his uncanny love for his latest victim, both men heard *it*. The noise of wet clay sounded as if it plopped on the floor in the bedroom across from them. Quick-breaths and ungodly moans of something unnatural and ominous emanated from the guest bedroom. The apprehensive resonance was like that of a dead person breathing fresh air into their newly functioning lungs and groaning through the discomforts of rigor mortis. Wet clumps plopped. No, wet plaster. That of a freshly built wall. Then the moans, one after another—some low and others hoarse. Soon came the alien sounds of something brushing (or dragging) upon the plush carpet from the other room.

Cole did not move. He was caught in a nightmare-inducing reverie between the man who threatened his life at the end of a blade and the enigma of what would become of the horrid tones that seemed to grow closer.

In relation, James was impaired of all movement. However, he still applied the razor tightly against his "love's" throat; his eyes were wide open to the horrors approaching. What was to come through that doorway was not natural, and he knew *it* was coming for him.

Moan.

Drag closer.

Shock!

A figure came tripping into the bedroom. It was that of a young man. With it, came the scent of deadened flesh and rot. The smell of gases and innards putridly embraced the atmosphere and killed out all other smells. The young corpse was bluish and still had the traces of a dried scarlet line across his neck. The purplish and brown veins showed through the flesh, near the eyes that were covered over with a translucent film that were absent of color. *Its* body twitched to a halt and waited.

Cole lay aghast in his trance; for he knew not what this was in front of him or why *it* was here. Desperately, he attempted to trace back where this nightmare had begun. Although, he could focus on nothing save for the apparition in front of him. Ghost in front of him? Creature? Zombie?

On the other hand, James knew. Oh God, he knew more than ever. After all, he had indeed seen this boy before, right before picking up Cole. And he knew this boy's name was Geoff. And he was sure he had murdered him. And he wanted ever so much to believe this was fiction standing before him.

"J--AAA--MMM--ES," the zombie groaned in a low, broken voice as he pointed a convulsing finger at his assailant.

What exploded James' heart into a song of massive panic, more amusing than any classical crescendo he had ever heard, was the site of what slowly followed behind the creature. What unsteadily bobbed into the room next, like a hellish jack-in-a-box on bent spring, was another creature that James recognized as Christopher. Christopher's flesh was pale compared to that of his undead companion. Gray and white splotches covered his naked flesh that dangled from his arms and chin. James observed a piece tear from the foot that the creature drug behind and make home to the carpet. This unholy apparition pointed a wavering finger at his killer and spoke his name in unholy invocation. Two more from behind Christopher's corpse emerged, barely able to balance in their traipse of the undead. Dale and Gary. They both appeared the same, as hollowed skeletons, bones yellowed from aching decay. Their skull mouths opened as to say his name as well, and skeletal fingers made an apprehensive gesture toward him.

A hydrogen bomb of utter trepidation exploded and devastated Cole's rational mind. Quickly, he fell into a state of unconsciousness. He abruptly fainted, head rolling to the left, and his tender neck became minutely slit from the pressure James' threatening razor.

James eagerly shoved Cole's benumbed body away from his own and off the bed, throwing it to the floor. He leapt off the bed waving his razor at all of his once victims that had returned for an obvious revenge. Geoff, Christopher, Dale, Gary—all his victims that were once beautiful were now horrific monsters that stood before him with accusing fingers.

"Stop it. Leave. GET OUT," he yelled.

"But.....I love.....you, James," the freshest carcass rebutted.

"Yes, James," Christopher's withering face replied, "I love you too."

"We love you, James," the other two skeletal remains reported, mocking in tones gurgling and high-pitched.

A festival of horrendous laughter and dreadful 'I love yous' timbered throughout the bedroom. Hoarse, high-toned, gurgling and demonic. The freak show of gory passion approached James, swaying and jerking as their puppet master of reverence guided them. They were dead marionettes controlled by evil, Karma, and Fate. Mostly, they were hell-bent on avenging their deaths.

"Stay away," James cried out, waving his straight razor at the zombified cadavers.

"We love—"

And the carcass of Christopher continued on with the awe-striking statement, "Yes, James we—"

"Love you," the osseous frameworks finished off, as if they were mentally connected to one another.

"No.....get away," James screamed at the top of his lungs, exasperating all breath and almost sounding like a teenage girl. "Nooooooo...noooooooooo!"

Christopher's body of cold meat swatted his arm. James could hear the terrible crunching sounds of rigor mortis. The zombie's dead hand knocked the razor from his hand. It landed between the bed and wall, directly near Cole's oblivious figure.

The two skeletal remains wobbled and wiggled like Jell-O towards James and grabbed him from either side. James tried resisting, feeling the dry and bony fingers grip tightly with inhuman strength to his forearms. Writhing in frantic escape, James tried moving backward and forward. However, the undead had a massive grasp on him and would not allow any exit but that which would lead to Hell.

The chemical stimulus thwarting throughout his existence consisted of impossible horror and pitiful regret. Then he studied, when he realized he had no other option but to submit to this frenzy, as the animated deadness of Christopher stumbled behind him and grabbed on to his waist. Finally, Geoff was in front of him and placed his hands on either side of his face, as if to kiss him deeply.

The four monsters yanked at James with all their might. James screeched in absolute consternation. He felt the agony that emitted from his shoulders as the skeletons pulled on his arms, disjointing them. Searing with pain, he shrilled as his waist was being toiled from behind. Geoff twisted with its subhuman strength at James' head, wrenching it to the left and right, as if it were a cork pulled from a bottle of blood red wine.

Flaring pain engulfed James' being. Flaring, then the appalling sounds of that of paper being frayed; flesh stretching to the point of tearing. His eyes rolled up as he felt the pressure of his embodied blood spurt from his arms, waist, and head. Stretching. Wrenching. Dismemberment of his body. And as he felt the blood shed and his limbs dissect from his body, the last thought was not that of love, but of inconceivable terror.

***

"I don't want to die," Cole incoherently murmured as he came to. The residuals of the wine kept his mind buzzed. He glanced to his contorted figure and saw the straight razor with a droplet of blood staining its gleam. Suddenly, it all came back to him—his virus, James trying to kill him, and.....monsters?

He beamed up to find a room full of cadavers that lay about the bedroom floor. They were grotesquely piled, as if they had fallen upon one another in a collection of decay. Cole gagged when the smell of rotten flesh and coppery blood reached his nostrils. Upon the bed, he made a gruesome discovery.

James' head was placed in the middle of the bed. Shreds of flesh dangled from the neck as crimson plasma oozed in a puddle of gore. His eyelids were half-open; his eyes rolled back into their sockets. The tongue that had entangled with Cole's earlier, sickly parted his teeth and was resting halfway out of his mouth. The remainder of his body was strewn about the room like a rag doll.

Cole was insanely flabbergasted by the unholy site. The monsters wouldn't get him though, for they lay dead. Those zombies and their vengeful, murdersome hands that had taken James from this world were now nothing but mysterious corpses to be discovered by a neighbor that would, within days, complain about the rank smell that emitted from this chamber of horror.

Cole sadly realized, was he not the same? He was no different from the creatures he had seen. Yes, they had died and returned to the living, but he was the walking dead as well. *Walking through life with this deadly virus.* How could he live with this horrible affliction that would kill him in the near future?

He recalled his fear of death, his pleas to the world to live and be healthy. Yet, was it not better to die a quick death than a slow one? Eventually, he would become a zombie too, for his body would slowly decompose. And with that idea at hand, Cole grasped the straight razor and finished tracing the line upon his neck that James had started. If not for death, he could not be free.

Everlong

It begins with the soothing touch of Damien's fingers upon my lips, and I cannot believe how real they feel! Ah, those fingers and how I know them well—the way I would suckle at them as the sleek tips played with my lower lip; and how I would beg for them as they eagerly entered my ass, propelling me into permissible rapture. They are, like the rest of Damien's flesh, a fountain bursting with silken texture.

Touch.

It feels all too familiar and, yet, it reveals a deep mystery before my eyes. For I've never known his touch like this before, never thought of how it would feel for ectoplasm and flesh to blend in sync. It's like a sponge soaked in water—wet, saturated, and full-bodied. Honestly, I wouldn't think it possible and could easily chock it up to the ravings of a madman obsessed by love. But I know it's happening now. Our vows were spoken, and we have each other in the here and now the way we promised.

Damien's love for me is strong, as he places his hands on either side of my face and pulls me forward. I cannot resist; I have no strength to assert otherwise. His voluptuous, bee-sting lips cover my mouth as our tongues wildly dance in a wicked rhythm of driven beats like those to which we had danced at the many after-hour clubs in the first year we were together. His tongue fervently slides down my throat and I use all my will to grab hold of his precious, Roman face to pull him back. Yet, I love the sensation of our tongues twisting together, and the solace and solidity it brings to our bond.

Damien draws back and curiously stares at me with emerald eyes that accentuate his disheveled, russet hair.

I want to speak, but it seems superfluous. Nevertheless, I make an attempt in hopes that he will hear my words. "I love you," I state.

His eyes pierce mine as he says, "I know Talon. I love you too." His soft-spoken voice echoes in the room all around me.

This was once our bedroom. This was once our home.

***

Three months after Damien and I had married, we had taken our habitual nightly walk after a late dinner. Damien had always loved going for walks after a full meal. Not that he needed to lose weight, mind you.

After all, Damien's tall frame was built like that of a swimmer. It didn't matter if I cooked one of my favorite homemade Italian dishes or if we grabbed fast food takeout; Damien never gained a pound. He had a metabolism for which any gay man would die!

But that wasn't why I fell in love with Damien. For the two of us, though a handsome couple, looked beyond the surface of each other's bodies. The man I fell in love with, and ultimately married, was friendly to everyone he encountered. He had a warm smile that could easily entice the most inattentive stranger. And I was never jealous of the charisma Damien exuded because it was that of a caring man, that of one who could solace the saddest of souls. He also shared many of the passions as I had (one of them being that of discovering fine restaurants with which we could share meals and each other's company).

Damien found, in me, a similar man that mirrored himself (though I was an inch shorter than he, with jet-black hair that spilled over the nape of my neck). I was neither skinny nor overweight; I was simply height/weight proportionate. This shocked both Damien and me, as I had a flair for regularly cooking pasta recipes passed down through my Italian lineage. That was one of the reasons why Damien felt it necessary to take an evening stroll. He did so to burn off all the carbohydrates with which we had induced during dinner. Later in the evening, we'd find many more pleasurable ways to burn off the calories.

Who was it that said, 'opposites attract?' Curiously, that did not apply to Damien and me. We were almost carbon copies of each other, with the same interests and driven passions. We were together for a little over a year and a half before we walked down the aisle to say our "I do's." During that point in time, when we gazed into each other's eyes and married each other's soul, we found that it was going to last forever.

We ambled through the historical, Willo District, hands clasped. We usually conversed very little as we made our course around the area. It was visually pleasing to pass the ancient homes in our neighborhood that boasted primitive architecture and differentiated from the models of the modern, cookie-cutter homes built throughout the rest of Phoenix. Our downtown residence provided a view of the past, while the steel and glass towers of the modern, corporate world loomed over the vicinity.

As we were about to come full circle to the street on which our own historical home was located, I noticed two men walking toward us. One was an overweight Hispanic man with a straggly mullet haircut. The other was a gangly man of which a red, cotton bandana covered his head. Both men appeared drunk as they staggered onward and wildly laughed.

When they spotted us, they whispered something unintelligible and drew close with staid expressions carved upon their faces.

My gut reaction was that these two men were trouble, or they were out looking for it. As they approached us, my stomach folded and my heart skipped a beat. Damien's sweaty palm tightly gripped my hand.

***

Damien and I fall back upon our bed and, together, our bodies feel weightless, as if gravity has sacrificed itself, yet again, for our carnal pleasure. His tongue continues probing my mouth, pushing past my own tongue and invading my throat. It feels as if it could go through the nape of my neck if it was long enough. My hands roam down the curve of his back, as the veritable sensation of either beads of sweat or spectral substance dampens my fingers.

Pulling his tongue from my mouth, Damien gently kisses my lower lip that quivers from his touch. He licks at my chin, and then creates a wet trail as his tongues glides down my neck and to the crevice between my pectorals. Damien maneuvers his licking to my right nipple. His tongue makes slow, sensual circles around it before he gives it a playful bite. I want to moan from this ecstasy, but a new jubilation overwhelms me as Damien's mouth makes it way over my trembling stomach and glides over my solid cock. I delightfully gasp as Damien's mouth swallows my entire organ. I almost erupt from the warm fluids of his gulping.

I feel Damien's wonderful fingers as they tenderly enter my anus and tease my prostate. All the while, he continues sucking my pulsing cock as my insides explode with euphoria. Damien pins both of my hands against the bed as he interlaces his fingers with mine before I have a chance to recover from this rapture. Mentally knowing how badly I want him inside of me, I gratefully experience Damien's own rigid cock as it enters me. His slow, rhythmic thrusting launches my body into a netherworld unlike I've ever known. My neck arches back and my head feels as if there is nothing beneath it. There is no bed, no floor. There is no room, only empty space. Our lovemaking is like floating. Our surroundings are made up of fluids, bliss, and love everlasting.

***

We halted in our tracks as the two men stood before us. The one with the bandana on his head had bloodshot eyes. His pockmarked face was well aged beyond his actual years, evidently a product of excess drinking and drug use. He looked over to his Hispanic friend and hoarsely asked, "What the fuck do we have here?"

The Hispanic man answered, "Looks like two *maricons* to me, eh?" He stared at me. I noticed the fine hairs of his thin mustache ended halfway down his upper lip.

Bandana-man glared at Damien and then me. "Is that what we have, a couple of faggots?"

Damien stood stock-still and silent. I, on the other hand, was not going to take any shit. "So what of it?"

"Damn, *esse*, you seem to have an attitude."

"He sure does, doesn't he?" The man with the bandana on his head stared into my soul with contempt.

Back to the Hispanic man who had greasy hair that gleamed beneath the streetlights. "Why you two holding hands like that in public and shit? You know you're just asking for trouble."

"Isn't that what married couples do?" I asked.

The two men's guffaws infiltrated the quiet night. Their laughter was like that of lunatics, and that thought caused the adrenaline to race throughout my body and my heart to hammer in my chest.

"Talon," Damien called as he inched me closer to him as if to make a way around the two thugs.

"Talon?" The foreigner mocked and looked to his buddy.

"Sounds like a faggot name to me," he commented. It triggered more laughter from the two.

Soon, their hilarity died out. They stepped in the direction in which Damien was trying to pull me.

"So, you two s'posed to be married and shit?"

"Men don't get married," the lanky one stated.

"They do now," I proudly declared.

"So who's the 'bitch'?" the Hispanic queried in his sharp, Mexican accent.

"Yeah," the man with the bandana yelled in hatred, "who wants to be the fucking widow?" He reached into the back of his worn jeans and extracted a long, shiny stiletto. The look in his eyes spoke of chaos and judgment; the sardonic expression upon his face screamed of revulsion.

Damien gasped. I looked over to see his eyes bulged in apprehension. I had never witnessed my partner that frightened before, and he appeared an unknown stranger to me.

From the corner of my eye, the gleam of the stiletto briefly blinded me. The glare disappeared and I felt an abrupt twist fill my gut. I wheezed for air as I directed my attention from Damien to my stomach and discovered the hand of my aggressor pulling up upon the golden handle of the knife. As he extracted it from my flesh, a crimson gore surged and soaked my shirt. Another jab of the blade eagerly assaulted my viscera and was rapidly jerked out. My body burst with agony; my nerve endings were set afire by terror. As I fell to my knees, I lost grip of Damien's hand. My head cracked against the balmy asphalt of the street as Damien cried out.

I gave one final glance to Damien and coughed up the word 'run,' as I felt a warm wetness spill over my lips. Soon, everything faded and the world ceased to exist.

***

With one forceful, final thrust, Damien erupts inside of me. Every particle of my ghostly being tingles and I want to laugh and cry at the same time. Not a second later, cum shoots from my cock and arcs high above us. Before it can land onto my chest, it disintegrates midair like a pale glitter. Damien pulls himself out of my translucent form and a quavering sensation washes over me. I know that those who are truly in love can only achieve such sensitivity.

"I love you Talon," Damien whispers as he turns off the bedside lamp.
"I know"
I lie next to my husband as I listen to his sleep-induced, heavy breathing. I think of his corporeal touch and his vow to love me always and forever.

Being Human

I face a horror of which I have never known, a terrifying force that can easily destroy anything without regret.

It's beyond mad, the way they can lovingly touch you one moment, then suddenly strike you down as if they have lost all emotion tied to sanity. Then again, what is sanity? When is it that the boundaries of sanity are crossed and the inviting arms of madness recruit? What's more, what is it that transforms one to commit such vile acts?

Perhaps the metamorphosis begins with me.

It hurts. The pain is practically unbearable. The blood juts from Danny's severed forearm. The crimson color sprays along the floor and wall like a gory collage created by some magnificent, abstract artist. There is the binding pressure of build up, and then comes the release that spews upon the foundation of the room where Danny lays. A pinpricking accompanies the agony as the right half of the upper torso begins to go numb.

I've always liked Danny, my mind reminisces so that it can thwart the oncoming torture of the next blow.

Danny was the comic in our group. He was the guy who could always take a serious situation and turn it into a festival of laughter. I remember the one time Carey was distraught over his first time getting an HIV test. Danny pointed out that it was usually the cautious ones who caught the virus on the one night they were not practicing safe sex, not the promiscuous "whores" like Carey. Danny added that even if Carey died young, no other gay man would be able to top his record of sexual conquests. We had all laughed at that particular remark. Thankfully, Carey's test results came back negative.

Evan, it's all your fault!

A gleam ignites the dim-lit room of the cabin as the lamp reflects the shiny head of the axe held high over Evan's head. Evan swings the axe downward and lands it into the pit of Danny's stomach. Two geysers of blood shoot from either side of Danny's abdominal area as the cold blade touches his warm innards.

I gag as the vomit rushes into the back of my throat. I want to scream. *Where the hell did you get an axe anyway? And why did you come to the cabin?*

Danny takes deep gulps as he attempts to gasp for air. A syrupy, cherry-colored pool erupts from his mouth. He chokes on the blood as he takes in another breath. It spurts into the air and on to Evan's jeans.

Carey stands in the corner of the room, and his jaw is practically to the floor. Earlier he roared, "Evan, what the fuck are you doing?" Now, his eyes are bulged in fright, unable to comprehend all that is happening. Still, as much as he can run from this place, he is staring at Danny's dismembered and dying body.

I see Carey's hazel eyes. They have always captivated me.

"Do it again, Evan. Take off the head," Billy instructs.

Billy was always the odd one, the one who delved into the mysterious ideas of the occult. So it comes as no surprise that he knows what he is doing.

Another choke of blood erupts from Danny as Evan raises the bloodstained axe.

I have to get out of here. I won't make it through this. It's too much!

Before the final blow comes—before Danny's head separates from the rest of his youthful body—his eyes catch glimpse of Carey's hazel irises. For a moment, everything goes black. Surely, that is the way it's supposed to happen.

-2-

It was always Evan. It hadn't mattered to me that there was a decade of friendship between us. In actuality, that made it feel even more right—the fact that we had survived the turmoil of drunken arguments and vicious gossip between acquaintances. Friends go through that.

I had met Evan in Junior High. Although I wasn't sure of my sexuality at the time, there was something about Evan that mesmerized me. Perhaps it was his brilliant green eyes, the way in which they pierced deep into my soul from behind the shocks of Evan's black hair. It may have been the way his cheekbones sat high and accentuated an oval face that would become, in his adult years, hatchet sharp. Nonetheless, I had instantly befriended him the day we sat next to each other in the Advanced Algebra class that we had both attended. Evan had a question about the multiplication of exponents, and I was more than eager to help him.

That very day that I had assisted Evan with the complexities of Algebra, he had invited me back to his place. I remember that day (though ten years ago) as if it were yesterday.

We climbed the staircase to his bedroom. It was a Friday and his mother and father were on vacation for the weekend. They had left him a hundred bucks! Imagine—a fifteen-year-old with a hundred dollars to spend for the weekend! Evan had asked me to stay the night, and I immediately obliged by contacting my mom and letting her know I was doing so.

Mom never had a problem trusting my decisions. She'd always said, "Dustin, you're going to have to be responsible some day, and there's no time like the present. Just, be careful." I sometimes wondered if the latter comment revealed that my mother had known I was gay. It had sounded as if she were the unwilling victim to the public service announcements that incessantly boasted the dangers of unsafe sex.

Evan popped in a movie and turned off the light in his bedroom. The title of the movie appeared to fly out of the screen in silence to announce *The Evil Dead*. I had never been a big fan of horror movies. They usually scared the living daylights out of me. Nonetheless, I sat with my back against the foot of Evan's bed as I watched the opening sequence involving an Oldsmobile Delta 88 making a slow crawl toward a deserted cabin.

A flame had ignited within the room, and my attention immediately turned to Evan. He had lit what I thought to be a cigarette. Evan sucked on the end, taking as much of the smoke as he could into his lungs. He held it in. "Want a hit, Dustin," he had tried speaking without letting the smoke escape from his lungs.

"I don't smoke cigarettes," I had replied.

Evan exhaled, and a stream of smoke made its way toward me. "It's not a cigarette. It's a joint." Evan had extended his hand toward mine. The joint had been tightly pressed between his thumb and index finger. After a few seconds, Evan had brought the joint back to his thin lips.

I had never smoked marijuana before. However, there was something about that particular moment that had occurred before my eyes. Evan's lips had continuously touched the end of the joint. There had been a yearning within me, a ravenous beast of lust, that wanted nothing more to touch my lips to Evan's. Yet, I was afraid to make such a move. Evan seemed so masculine in his demeanor, and the last thing I wanted to do was scare him off or give him any reason to dislike me.

Giddiness filled my stomach just by being around Evan. Nevertheless, I had to know him better. I had to make sure he liked guys too. So, instead of kissing him, I accepted the joint from Evan and tightly pursed my lips to the end. I had touched my lips to the same crinkled paper to which Evan had touched his. I had been instantly filled with delight! As the smoke entered my lungs, I had imagined that it was Evan. In that same moment, I had thought of the word 'soulmate.'

That night, we laughed our asses off.

-3-

Carey's eyes are wide open, as if he is forcing himself to stay awake. He stands, straddling the wall, a leg on either side, as he listens to Evan and Billy's impossible conversation.

Evan throws his hands into the air, revealing forearms sprinkled in blood. In fact, Evan is speckled in crimson gore from his flawless face to the cuffs of his denim jeans. It is Danny's blood.

Evan, you bastard! How could you kill one of your best friends?

"I can't believe it," Evan screams. *As if he is sorry.* Everyone saw him hold the axe high over his head. There was definitely the intent to kill with that powerful, downward swing. "Why is this happening?" Evan quickly turns away from Billy and towards Carey.

Carey immediately glances to the ground, intimidated by the feral look of Evan's squinting eyes.

"You tell me what the fuck is happening," Billy yells. "Why did we come to the cabin anyway?"

"You know why," Evan replies and pulls back his shoulders to loosen the tension building in his neck. "This is where he came. I promised his mother I would find him."

"Well fuck," Billy raises his voice again. His mouth is so wide open that the light of the room pronounces the gap between his teeth. "We fucking get here and Danny freaks! I mean, what the hell was he talking about? Why did he get up on you like that, Evan?"

Evan takes in a deep breath, and one can easily hear the shuddering roll past his lips. "I don't know. What did I do?"

"Did you see the color of his fucking eyes?" Billy hollers.

"I don't know what I saw," Evan denies.

"They were fucking black, man! He had the eyes of a goddamned demon!"

"No, no. I don't believe in that shit. All I know is that he came up on me talking crazy and I was gasping for air. I think he was choking me," Evan attempts to justify his actions.

"Bullshit," Carey interrupts the conversation. "He was trying to love you. But that's too deep for you, isn't it you whore?"

"Shut the fuck up, Carey," Billy demands.

"What are you talking about?" Evan inquires in a tone of helplessness.

"You," Carey raises his hand and points toward Evan. "You, the one who can fuck all your friends, but not give a damn about the one who loves you most."

Carey's accusation leaves Evan dumbfounded and speechless.

Carey's eyes come up to meet Evan's. Surely, they both see that the inky hue of night has eclipsed the once mesmerizing color of Carey's hazel irises.

"Look!" Billy is instantly frantic. "Give me the axe!" Billy scurries toward Evan.

"What are you doing?"

"His eyes, Evan! Look at his eyes."

They see it. I don't want to watch what happens next. But I have to. It all has to make sense! I'm not sure how much more of this I can take.

Billy controls the axe now. He pulls it to the right, far behind him, as his footfall races upon the wooden floorboards in Carey's direction.

Carey's arms stretch toward Billy with hands grappling for his throat. Billy's mouth goes agape at Carey's sudden roar of a scream. Carey's blackened scleras pierce deeply into the blue waters of Billy's eyes.

But Billy's oceanic irises are far from calm, for there are immense waves of destruction in those eyes. As he brings the axe full-force into the dead center of Carey's head, I think I see a faded spark.

Once again, there is a moment where darkness pervades the atmosphere and I begin feeling giddy. I want to vomit.

I can't believe it has come to this.

-4-

Evan and I had met Carey and Billy shortly after graduation. By that time, Evan and I were both out of the proverbial closet. We were young, gay men with a longing for all-night partying and sexual conquests.

Of course, my sexual experiences were limited to the guy who chose me only after Evan had left with somebody else. After all, Evan was the object of every gay man's desire. What with his chiseled face and defined torso, it was no wonder that, in a sea of club-going men brimming with lust, Evan was the epitome of sexual appetite.

Contrary to my boastful lies to Evan every day after such an encounter, he never knew that the previous night would usually end with my going home alone. And, for those who would hold my hand and follow me through the dimly lighted streets to my apartment, they were in for sheer disappointment. For when it came down to it—clothes hastily being thrown to the living room floor as tongues would wildly try to discover the hunger of love behind the salty taste of dirty martinis—I found that I would come to a halt and ask them to leave. I couldn't go through with it; for it was Evan's face that would come to mind. It was Evan's body that I would want pressed hard against mine. In my hopeful imaginings, the reality of the stranger before me would cause me to lose my drive. Always, before the door would slam shut, I was accosted with bitter accusations of being a cock-tease or a prude.

There had come a time when my feelings had been destroyed. That was the Sunday morning I had decided to surprise Evan with breakfast. Little did I know that I would be greeted by a scene of Evan sandwiched between Carey and Billy. They were fast asleep in a tangle of sheets and naked flesh. They appeared picturesque, as if an artistic collage of skin and muscle. At that point, I immediately (and silently) retreated from Evan's apartment. As the pit of my stomach folded over, I had made the hasty decision to extract the key to Evan's apartment from my key ring and place it in front of the door to his apartment.

My mind had raced in a frenzy I had never experienced and my heart seemed to have skipped beats. It had been as if every hope I ever had of being with Evan got violently stripped away in that one moment that incessantly played in my head to the rhythm of a skipping CD. It hadn't mattered, the times we shared. It hadn't mattered, the laughter we experienced while around each other. No, Evan having a threesome with two people we had known for nearly a year had summed it up. He had crushed my heart.

After three days of trying to contact me, I decided to answer Evan's call. That was the day when I had expressed my love for him.

-5-

"What the fuck, Billy?" Evan screeches in tones like that of a banshee.

Billy is knelt on one knee as he carefully observes the split in Carey's forehead. Scarlet rivers rush down either side of Carey's face and form a pool upon the hardwood floor of the cabin.

From Billy's mouth comes, "I had to. Did you see? He was one of them."

"No," Evan denies. "No, no, no, no, fucking no!" Evan is frantic as he paces, surely making his best attempt at not looking toward Danny and Carey's lifeless bodies adorning the floorboards with rivers of red hues found in nightmares.

"It's a dream; it's a fucked up dream," Evan grasps for rationalization.

"No," Billy speaks. You know what they were. What they became."

"Stop with your goddamned demon talk. There are no such things as demons you stupid fucker! We have to find Dustin! Please, let's find Dustin now and get the fuck out of here!"

It's the first time I hear my name being spoken by any of the quartet who only arrived fifteen minutes ago. *I don't want Evan to find me. No, not in that condition; not like that!*

"Dustin's mom said he was coming out to the cabin this weekend. You remember how she told us how worried she was about the way he's been acting this last year. I hadn't really noticed."

"Maybe he came out here so he couldn't be found," says Billy.

"No," Evan instantly refutes. "I'm one of his best friends. He'd want me to be here for him." Evan pauses for a moment. A sniffle permeates the gory silence of the blood dripping onto the crimson floor from the bodies of Danny and Carey.

"I think he's here," Billy claims.

"I think he is hiding from whatever is happening in this place."

"He's hiding all right. I know where he is, too."

Evan perks up. "You know where he is?"

"Yes," Billy speaks. "Are you sure you want to see him?"

"Stop speaking in riddles! Two of our friends have been murdered by us! Let's find Dustin and get the fuck out of here before something else happens. How are we going to explain any of this?"

Billy stands up and forcefully pulls the axe from Carey's head. A squishy sound erupts from the extraction of the axe. With Billy's back to Evan, Billy says, "C'mon" and exits the room.

I can hear Evan's footsteps behind Billy's as they seek me out.

-6-

It had been a year ago that I professed my love to Evan. I simply couldn't hold it in any longer. We had known each other for nearly a decade and had shared secrets, ostracized others beyond our own velvet rope, and had more in common that I had originally thought the first night I'd spent the evening at his house.

"But we're just friends," had been his answer.

His words had immediately defeated me. Still, I tried with all I had left in me to allow him to see what could come of such a relationship. "We could just go out on a couple of dates and see what happens. I'm not suggesting anything serious right away. If it doesn't work, so be it."

"Dustin, you have always been one of my best friends. I could never see you as anything more than that."

All hope had been lost; tossed into an abyss of love abandoned evermore like a child's tattered rag doll that has seen its last day.

I gave up.

-7-

I hear the floorboards creak with disdain as they experience the virginal footfall of Evan and Billy make their way through the two bedrooms and calling my name. After a lack of response, Billy directs Evan down the cabin's unusually long hallway to a closed door.

"I think he's in there," Billy suggests to Evan.

-8-

It was difficult spending time with Evan after he rejected me. I did my best to laugh at his jokes as we drank dirty martinis at a local bar. I held back in wanting to hold onto him during the scary movies we would watch at his apartment every other Thursday night. Most importantly, I refrained from wanting to move my mouth close to his lips, as I fell into his emerald eyes when we spoke face to face.

Thoughts of Evan sleeping with other guys (some with whom he had just met) had me going crazy. Not to mention, the fact that he continued sexual relationships with Danny, Carey, and Billy—my alleged friends—forced my brain into a state of craze of which I couldn't escape. I continued to think of Evan. Evan, the man I was meant to love for all time. Evan, the only man who I could've ever discussed about how I thought I did something wrong to my body the first time I masturbated in the shower. Evan, the man who slept with all of our friends but wouldn't dare lay eyes on me.

Two days ago, I told my mom I loved her and had to get away. She nodded in an understanding way in which only a mother can. She knew I was going to the family cabin up North. However, she couldn't have possibly imagined that the guest who accompanied me was...

-9-

Billy stands back as Evan pushes open the door to the bathroom. Billy observes the wince upon Evan's face, a result of the foul odor of rotted blood.

-10-

...a .38 caliber revolver.

-11-

Evan gasps.
"Dustin! No!"
Billy's eyes observe Evan run to my limp body. Tears stream down Evan's perfect face as he grabs hold of my corpse, still flexible because my suicide has taken place merely seven hours previous. Billy curiously studies Evan grabbing at his chest as Evan notices the single bullet hole to the middle of my forehead. Around it, the red, gray, and purple colors create a patchwork of strewn gore. Multiple, crusted streams of blood create a horrific facemask of which one may wear to a Halloween ball. Billy watches as Evan pulls me into his arms.
Ah, to be held by Evan. Such sweet solace in the midst of paused desire.
Evan's lips are close to my cheek, and I wish I could feel their malleability or the saliva that uncontrollably dribbles over them. I long to

taste the salty tears that run down his cheeks and near my mouth. *If just for a moment, yes!*

"Why did you do this, Dustin?"

Evan pauses as he takes in a deep breath and looks through watery eyes to Billy. "They did it to him, didn't they?"

"Who?"

"What you said...the demons."

Billy's body comes into the soft light of the bathroom. "Demons don't exist, Evan. But love does."

Evan squints to notice Billy's black eyes.

He has discovered me.

Billy's eyes study Evan as he stands and holds out a trembling, accusatory finger at Billy. "B-B-Billy. Your eyes," Evan's voice quavers.

"Yes. *My* eyes, Evan. And please call me Dustin."

I watch Evan's lips peel back from the terrifying revelation as he briskly gazes to my shell of a body upon the floor and back to my new form. "But...Dustin is—"

"Dead," I interject. "Actually, my body is dead. My soul, however, continues to live on."

"I don't understand." Evan is obviously perplexed, just as I was at first. He puts his back to the wall of the bathroom and creeps toward me, as if he is ready to bolt pass me.

"That's interesting, Evan. I didn't understand at first, either. Then it hit me like a ton of bricks. It's you, Evan. My soul continues to live because of my love for you. You do know I love you, right Evan?"

As I look down at Billy's hand (my hand) tightening the grip on the axe, Evan uses this opportunity to shove pass me. I pivot and observe Evan racing down the lengthy hall of the cabin, obviously en route to the front door. But he will not escape from me. He's been unable to do so since his arrival.

Just as Evan reaches the living room, a place where the carcasses of his two friends (whose bodies had been my earlier hosts) lay in growing puddles of blood, I heave the axe toward him. The heavy, butt end of the stainless steel strikes the back of his head, creating a solid thud sound, and Evan drops face first onto the wet, hardwood floor.

I grab the axe from next to Evan's body and kneel near him. As I turn him onto his back, I study the rivulets of blood that pour from his nose. I sit on top of his hips, keeping him pinned, and press the blade of the axe against the tender flesh of his throat. A red line develops from the pressure of the razor-sharp edge of the tool.

Evan's eyelids flutter open, and I am suddenly lost in those precious emeralds that I fell in love with a decade previous. I lean in close to kiss his lips, and he cringes from me, as if I a leper. "What? I'm not good enough for you? Billy's body isn't good enough for you? You had no problem fucking him before."

"Please," Evan whines. Tears form in his eyes, and I can feel his body trembling beneath me like that of a child afraid of the bogeyman. "Please...don't hurt...me." Evan sniffles.

"Hurt you? HURT *YOU*?" I scream into the air, yelling loud enough for false gods to hear my cries and curses. "*You* were the one who hurt *me*! You, always looking for the next pretty boy to fuck and never caring for the man who truly loved you. You, never able to process the concept of love because you were too busy in your world of plastic bodies and designer clothing. You, who could've had a long-lasting life with a man who would have given you the world! And you gave it up for what? The pleasures of casual sex? The greed of materialistic gain? You killed me when you said I was only a friend. You sealed my fate when you made it known that I wasn't good enough. I wasn't Danny or Carey or Billy or the numerous other men who came in and out of your life like cheap whores with one thing on their minds."

Evan's eyelids close. They are wet with tears because he understands the guilt I bestow upon him.

"I came here to kill myself because I could no longer take spending time with you every day and watching you go home with a new person from some club or bar every other night. But it didn't work, did it? Do you know why? I do.

"True love never dies, Evan," I explain. "Because of you, I killed myself. But my longing for you lived. In fact, your wrath has killed me two other times tonight. Danny. Carey. Still, I live. Now, I live in Billy. What will it take for you to understand that we were meant to be?"

Again, Evan's eyes open. *Love the green swirls of his irises, yes!* His eyes dart back and forth, as if seeking a quick solution. His panting has slowed. He seems calm, and his eyes meet mine.

"Will you love me forever, Dustin?"

I release the threatening blade of the axe from his neck and set the tool aside. I stare into his emerald irises and almost gasp as their color begins to fade, clouded by grays that will eventually turn black.

"Yes, Evan, I will," I declare.

With that, I feel Evan's clammy hands behind my neck, pulling my face down to his. We kiss. Our tongues dance in a psychotic romance of newfound lusts.

-12-

I face a horror of which I have never known, a terrifying force that can easily destroy anything without regret. Some call it love. I call it being human.

In an isolated cabin, far from the outcries of the city, Evan and I are naked and discovering the flesh of one another. The moonlit skies promise banshees and vampires while we eagerly roll around upon a floor that is wet and sticky with viscera, semen, and tears.

In the Shadow of Hades

Cammie nervously sits, unsure as to why the girls even invited her fat ass over in the first place. The videotape that plays in the old Magnavox VCR begins with Sabrina and Lily's bodies standing opposite one another, their eyes wide open and transfixed on each other. It's a cheap-made home video; the picture through the camera's lens is perfectly still, obviously sitting atop a tripod. Behind the confronting bodies of the two young women are the great gateways to the Pintlers, the tranquil wilderness of Anaconda, Montana. The glorious, green pines gently sway as the gelid October day brings with it a mild breeze. Given the outside lighting, the sky overhead is gray and overcast. It is the perfect setting for the phenomenon they are about to prove to Cammie, who only befriended the two last week. It was a week after she'd relocated to the town and into a house with her father who had won custody of her.

Within the dilapidated, one bedroom house that stands at the Pintler foothills, just on the most northern end of the town, where Seventh Street overlooks Locust, the three girls sit. Cammie twirls flaxen strands of her shoulder-length hair between her index and middle fingers, intently watching the television screen. The home video holds her interest as she watches the prelude to Sabrina and Lily's "supernatural game."

Possessor.

That's what the girls had called it. Supposedly, through deep meditation, Sabrina was going to take over Lily's body. They videotaped this eyewitness account last month so that they could prove it to whoever had doubted it. That doesn't mean much to Cammie. It could all be a hoax, but it was entertainment. What does matter is that the two girls are consorting with her and taking her into their clique. Why? Cammie doesn't know.

Sabrina and Lily sit pretty, across from their new friend. Sabrina glimpses over at Cammie, and then throws her attention back to Lily with a smirk of mischief, a smile that could be that of two teens playing a joke or two maniacs pre-meditating a diabolical murder.

Cammie studies the nineteen-inch, Sony television screen and observes the two attractive, young coeds. They are both beyond

Cammie's physical league. Sabrina has long and deep-colored, chocolate hair that blows gracefully in the wind, a hatchet-sharp face with glistening eyes and a supermodel smile. She is almost sickly thin like Lily whose wavy, blond hair frames a gorgeous, hollow-cheek face. The two girls are so beautiful standing opposite one other in the video; their eyelids are shut and reveal the softest blue-gray eye shadow. They are nothing like Cammie, and that's why she wonders why they took her in with friendliness. Cammie is forty pounds overweight, with a boy's haircut. Specks of acne scars plague her chubby face and quarter-inch bifocals shield her boring, gray eyes.

Cammie has always wanted to appear gorgeous like the girls, and feels uncomfortable around them. She questions their friendship sometimes. When she lies awake in her bed at night, touching herself about her large, flabby breasts and virginal zone, she can't help but wonder if the two girls are truly trying to be her friends or just using her as a scapegoat, an emotional punching bag. And Eric hasn't been around with his intuitive answers since she left Great Falls.

The two comely women on the videotape open their eyes to view one another.

Sabrina, the more naturally beautiful one speaks, "Are you ready?" It is a seductive voice that secretly turns Cammie on.

"I am ready," Lily responds, with her porcelain arms to her side.

"Are you ready?" Sabrina, once again, asks, her voice more amplified than before and carrying itself through the trees behind them.

"Yes," Lily states, with a stern sureness to her soft tone.

The two women bring the palms of their hands together high above, flesh touching flesh and silk consoling silk. They form an arch reminiscent of the childhood days of London Bridge. In unison, like the chant of a witches coven, they say, "We are ready. We are ready for Possessor."

A small chuckle arises in Cammie's throat. The chant reminds her of some cheesy, low-budget horror movie. She sways her head over to Sabrina and Lily who squint their eyes at her for mocking the video. "Sorry," Cammie hastily and insecurely apologizes.

"Watch," Lily anticipates, as if Cammie is not to miss one second of the video. "It's about ready to happen," she informs, speaking of the possession of her body to Sabrina's spirit.

Cammie redirects her attention to the screen and concentrates on the scene. Behind the arches of their arms, a small dove coos and flies off into the atmosphere. Obviously, a lost fledgling whose trip to the south was delayed. *How aesthetic the picture is,* Cammie thinks. Not the actual game itself, but the white feathers of purity that fly high above the wall of green forest. And the beauty of the two girls—how Cammie obsesses about looking as they do.

The dove flying, takes Cammie back in time, a time when Anaconda was just a place her father lived and Great Falls was a city full of preppies that mocked at her obesity like little children teasing classmates. The bird of peace takes her back to a time when she first met Eric.

***

The first night she made contact with Eric, her mother, Doris Hollerand, slapped Cammie's pudgy face. "You're fuckin' worthlesth," Doris slurred. She took another swig from the bottle of Jim Beam and almost gagged while swallowing the potent bourbon. "Ya don't have any goddamn friendsth and you sit on your fat assth all fuckin' day. You piece of sthit." Her rancid, alcohol breath was almost enough to get Cammie drunk off the overpowering fumes.

This was a common drama in the Hollerand, upper-story apartment, located in the small city of Great Falls. Doris was just pissed because her current boyfriend, Bachelor Number twenty-something, confessed that she was a fucking downer and he was banging the dental assistant next door in apartment 202. So it was Cammie who would feel the aftershocks of the arguments.

Cammie had no friends, not even in her senior class. She was a nerd, a fat slob at who the jock boys and the ruffian girls poked fun. There was not a single soul she could telephone in desperate hopes of her longed consoling. And Ted, her father, was gone for a week with his logging company. She hated those weeks, the weeks when she couldn't get a hold of her father, the times when he was absent from her life and with whom she couldn't confide her abused tears. He always knew how to give her hope by telling her that he was doing all he could with his lawyers to get custody of her and, one day, she would be living with him in Anaconda.

On that particular evening, the night of the hardest slap she had received in her life, upon entering her bedroom and switching on the light, a small, white dove was perched outside her window. She pressed her chubby face against the glass, her tears staining the inside along with snot. Through the entire upsetting ordeal, the dove refused to leave. It simply remained on the other side of the glass, pecking at the window with its tiny beak every couple of minutes, as if it heard her cries and was trying to relieve her.

When it flew away was when the voice of Eric made its presence.

Cammie had heard somewhere before that crows were carrions between the land of the dead and the living. Perhaps Eric was some type of guardian brought from his sacred land by the dove. She never discounted the voice of Eric as a sign of going insane, but as an audible and keen intuition. Eric had a deep, pleasant voice. It made its visit to her during all ordeals and, usually, before she made any rash decisions.

That night he said, *"You'll be fine, Angel."* What made her feel more special than anything was that he called her 'Angel.' Eric immediately became a second father to Cammie, the loving figure that was there when her real one was absent. Sometimes she visualized that it was actually her father telepathically calling out to her.

Whatever the case, Eric was always there before any impending danger. *"Go to your room, Angel,"* the inner voice had spoken before Doris went ballistic during her drinking binges. On another occasion, Eric had informed her, *"Watch out, Angel. Be careful of Sally Rothberg."* An hour later, she overheard one of her fluffy classmates brag about how Sally was going to 'kick that fat narc's ass.'

The last time Cammie had heard from Eric was right before her father called that late, September afternoon. That was the day that changed her abused, routine life. *"Hey, Angel. You're father's going to call. Pack your bags; this is what you've wanted."* Cammie had half her wardrobe in her suitcase by the time her father called to notify that he had won custody of her and he was coming to pick her up.

No, she had not heard from Eric since that day. That was the day she crossed the borders of Anaconda, a town that she felt somehow disturbed her intuition. What was it about this town?

***

"I—" Lily speaks on the video. She hesitates and, at the same time, concentrates on her every breath. She shuts her eyelids tightly. "I—," she pauses, "am—"

Sabrina stands beside Lily and whispers words barely audible to the microphone of the camcorder. The words come out quickly, repeating, during Lily's concentration. The words that fleet past Sabrina's thin lips are: "I am Possessor...I am Possessor...I am Possessor..."

Cammie gapes at the video, awaiting the bragged phenomenon to happen. Why are they showing her this anyway?

The scene replays—Lily's verbal focus on the 'I's and 'AM's and Sabrina's whispers flow beneath Lily's like the driving melody of a hard rock song.

"I—"

"AM—"

Then, finally, the last word, the word that seals the game's end, stems from Lily's mouth. The word both ladies end with is, "POSSESSOR."

When the word rolls over Lily's lips, Cammie notices that it is in the sexual tones of a compassionate voice. Was Sabrina actually in Lily's body, using her as a vessel? Then, from Lily's mouth comes, "I am Sabrina."

"I am Lily," Sabrina's confirms.

Cammie sits in awe. The two had actually swapped bodies! Cammie becomes fascinated by the concept. She imagines herself as thin and lovely as the two girls with their perfect curves. What she wouldn't do to swap bodies with somebody else!

The untelevised Sabrina examines the fat girl's expression of wonder. Cammie has obviously bought the idea; the video worked like a charm. The next step is to play the game. Yes, that was it. *Possessor* will seal Cammie's fate and lend another year of life to Sabrina and Lily, a gift for their sacrifice. It is their reward from the underworld.

Lily focuses her total attention on Cammie. "Well, are you ready to try it?"

Anticipating, Cammie's heart falls upon the slight rhythm of a pitter-patter. *That's why they wanted me to watch the video!* Although Cammie feels a bit nervous, body involuntarily trembling as if she's downed a half dozen cups of coffee, she cannot help but feel overwhelmed by the ordeal. This was her chance to look good for once and, if it were only for a brief moment, only for the slightest of seconds that she could view her idea of a perfect body, it would be worth it. That's right, in that magical moment, not a single person will taunt her or call her a 'fat bitch' or even make fun of her inflated, ugly face. This, indeed, was to be bliss for her.

"Sure, let's do it," Cammie eagerly responds.

With that, Lily acknowledges Sabrina and stands, extending her hand to Sabrina. The girl's best friend grasps the hand that reaches out to her and rises from the plush sofa. She plants a charming kiss upon Lily's mouth. "Let's head to the back," Sabrina says, motioning to Cammie.

As Cammie gets up, she can't help but wonder if the relationship between her two newfound friends is exactly platonic. She witnesses them kissing all the time and, when they go anywhere, they hold each other's hand. Sometimes, when they sit outside on the lawn talking with Cammie, they hold each other in an emotional embrace. While walking to Daly's convenient store down Maple Street last week, a car full of teenage girls yelled the term 'lesbians' at Sabrina and Lily.

Cammie doesn't care if the two girls are lovers. Although, the idea does provoke a sense of fear within her. The cliché thought of AIDS swims through her mind that is absent of any sexual education or experience. On the other hand, the lesbian claim helps her to feel more comfortable, for now she isn't the only one being teased.

The trio saunter out of the back door of the small home; Sabrina and Lily hold hands and Cammie follows closely behind. They head toward the wilderness, to a clearing that reaches beyond the two girls' open backyard, bordered by neither chain link nor wooden fences.

As they walk, the two lovers glance down to the fading, green blades of grass upon which they trod. Beneath the grass is another world. Beneath the earthen foundation is a dark place that calls to the two conspirators that Cammie follows. Lily senses the power, sensations, and awesome images that come from beneath her feet. It is a memory she chooses not to have, a recollection of a place in which she and Sabrina will return should they not present the gods a sacrifice.

Hades.....

***

Stone pillars of darkest marble plague the evil underworld. Cracked, uneven cobblestone covers the foundation. Flames within great cauldrons of fire surge and depress in pain-fulfilling threats to the souls that inhabit the land of suffering. The tallest of pewter-colored, cement walls create labyrinths and the withering vines, which were probably ripe and fresh when stripped from the Garden of Eden, decorate the barricades that run wildly throughout the netherworld. The biosphere's constant smells are the pungent vapors of decomposing viscera, charring flesh, and a peculiar smell of oil burning. Skies above are jet black and blinding whips of lightening bolts endlessly arc from the murky atmosphere; it's as if the air above is the electric source and the world below is a grand invention crafted by the creative hands of Nikola Tesla. Miniature, translucent clouds materialize and disappear among the mazy plain— souls of the unfortunate that have made their way here. Their ectoplasmic flesh hopelessly walks, beyond lost. The souls that get the privilege of vanishing from the wicked land do not escape; they only strike deals to grant them their own hells on Earth.

Such was the case with two attractive, young women who horrifically found their way to Hades two years previous. Their untimely demise was a result of a suicide pact between two lovers who couldn't cope with the outside world. Two, who were taunted by Anaconda's homophobic society and felt they had no choice but to slash the wrists of each other with Lady Gillette razors. First, there was the professing of their love to one another. Then, the slicing began—blood poured from the crook of their arms to the palm of their hands, red rivers over porcelain hands. Finally, there came the bleak darksome that they so much longed for. Through their black holes of death, they materialized in Hades just as if they walked through a dimensional doorway. The realization of the horror they witnessed in this wretched place was worse than any name-calling they had ever experienced. A single horned god did not greet their fear-induced, fragile souls. Instead, invisible gods that roared with thunderous, baritone voices welcomed them.

They were not in Hell or Purgatory. No, those places were grade school playgrounds in comparison to Hades. They were below Hell, planted deeper near the Earth's core. Hell was a few steps up the spiritual staircase; it was Heaven from the perspective of Hades. This place was where the lost and damned souls went. And the two women had surely damned their souls with their suicidal escape from life. However, they were given a choice. Their immortal souls could spend eternity in this place, everlastingly roaming the corridors of the Dark World, or the two had the option of returning to the Earth plain and living as the undead, provided they sacrificed another human on the annual celebration of their death.

A decision was quickly made; after all, who on Earth would subject themselves to such masochism? Sabrina and Lily returned to their home, both flabbergasted for days after the uncanny event. Since that day, the two viewed life in a different and darker light. The streets of Anaconda was to be the hunting grounds for their future prey as a piece of Hades' garden lingered in their world, casting its otherworldly shadow over their.....

***

.....fates.

Lily shivers in remembrance. Like a telepathic twinge that travels from her gray matter, throughout her muscles and to her fingertips, Sabrina peers at her living dead girl with concerned emeralds. Her own arm begins to spasm and she doesn't have to wonder what is going through Lily's head. *Yes, the time has come,* she thinks.

Coo. Coo.

The soft sounds of a dove emit high from the semi-circle of Pines that the trio enters. The grounds are barren, save for dead, yellowing branches and large rocks. The smell of Christmas is in the air, an aroma of giving gifts.

Elated and overexcited to play *Possessor,* Cammie searches the branches above for the dove's cry. Somewhere in the towering pine trees is Eric. Although she cannot find the peaceful bird, she hears Eric's tender voice. If only he could see her once she inhabits the body of either Sabrina or Lily.

"What are you doing, Angel?"

Cammie has no time to respond to Eric's concern since she is paying close attention as Sabrina begins projecting the events about to take place. "This is the place, Cammie," she announces. "It is here that you will take part in *Possessor*."

"Cool," Cammie responds like a small child finding a new toy. This was the moment she had come to anticipate.

"C'mon, Cammie," Lily calls. "Come join us here and form a circle."

Cammie approaches the two who are still holding hands. When she reaches them, Sabrina directs her to grasp her and Lily's hands. Cammie's palms begin to sweat. The touch of the delicate dolls is precious to Cammie's flesh. She had never been blessed by the soothing touch of such women. Not even from her mother, Doris; only the hard, popping slaps from that woman!

"Close your eyes and clear your mind," Sabrina requests. "Let nothing enter your mind but one word and that word is *Possessor*. No images may come to your mind; it should be completely blank."

Cammie begins making all the pictures in her mind dissipate into nothingness. The pretty faces of Sabrina and Lily disintegrate into a fading blur turning black. She shortly stalls her breathing, for the peaceful aromas of the wilderness fill her mind with mental pictures of pine trees and elk and squirrels (*and does*). All the snapshots begin to fade into indistinct shapes and, before long, the forms become nonexistent. There are no traces, not a single blemish; just an empty, inky gap. Darkness, then the faint calling of a gentle voice.

"*Angel*," it strives to communicate.

Interference. Clear. Mind becoming unhampered.

The voice echoes further away, like a person pursuing the deeper end of a cave, before Cammie gets a chance to recognize it from her stages of meditation.

"*Angel...*" it attempts to warn.

Static. Sounds fading.

"*...Don't—*"

Mind empty. Closed.

Cammie reaches her alpha state and silence pervades her thoughts. There is not a single disturbance—no girls yelling obscenities at her, no portrayals of the variation between beautiful and ugly. All that is left is a shared readiness by all three women.

Sabrina pops her eyelids open. "Are you ready?" she calls out to Lily and Cammie.

The two followers bring their surroundings into view. "We are ready," they respond in unison. Cammie instantly remembers the videotape, and then wipes the mental picture from sight.

The trio brings their palms together high in the air and pronounces aloud, "We are ready. We are ready for *Possessor*."

"Cammie Hollerand," Sabrina summons; her words ring loud up to the pinnacles of the trees and below to the underworld of Hades at the same time.

"Yeah, Sabrina," Cammie confirms. She suddenly feels awkward and a bit stupid. Hearing her own response makes her sound as if she worships the woman who calls her name.

Lily takes a couple paces back from the other girls.

"You are to lie upon Mother Earth's floor, Cammie," Sabrina instructs. "Lie on the ground and close your eyes. Speak the words that will direct your spirit into me."

Mother Earth? Cammie ponders. It appears to Cammie that Sabrina sounds more like somebody practicing witchcraft then playing a game. Regardless of her queer notion, she obeys and lies upon the landscape of the forest. She sniffles as the chilling air causes her nose to run.

Overall, the chubby Ms. Hollerand is excited. In just a short time, her spirit, her inner self, will transfer into the ravishing Sabrina Eckert. On the other hand, she isn't so sure if Sabrina will like the exchange of bodies. Who wants to be fat? Perhaps this was a way for Sabrina and Lily to give her a glimpse of self-confidence. Cammie appreciates that of her two friends. *What is Lily's part in the game anyway?*

Sabrina gives Lily one final glance, a nod of plans beginning. "You may begin, Cammie."

"I—" Cammie squeals aloud and takes in a deep breath.

Sabrina begins her chanting. "I am Possessor...I am Possessor...I am Possessor..."

"I—" the innocent, fat girl continues. "I am—"

"I am Possessor...I am Possessor...I AM POSSESSOR..." Sabrina emphasizes loudly on the last chant, making indications with her eyes to Lily.

Lily leans over and picks up an enormous boulder slightly embedded in the forest dirt. The rock is the size of a bowling ball, and is weathered with jags and etches. Lily strains as she lifts the granite up with both hands, the veins in her scrawny arms peer through her wan skin. She has only to haul it six feet to Cammie. and starts toward that direction. Lily swings the boulder with each slow step between her legs to maintain her balance.

"I—"

"...I am Possessor...I am Possessor...I am Possessor..."

"Am—"

"...I am Possessor...I am Possessor...I am Possessor..."

Lily is a foot away from Cammie; her weapon in hands is ready to fall.

Sabrina's eyes squint in anxiousness and malice, eyes of a traitor, and she is certain she hears the rumbling of the impatient gods in Hades, awaiting the girls' sacrifice. *Awaiting Cammie.*

Cammie's eyes remain sealed as she senses the final words drawing near from her voice.

Various sounds start flooding her mind. She hears Sabrina's constant chant. She hears the fast flickering of her own heart. The rustling of crispy, fall leaves invades her reddened ears.

"I—"

Coo. Coo.

"AM—"

"Angel, it's a trick! Don't"

"POSSESSOR." Cammie's final bellow is in unison with the last word of Sabrina's chant.

Cammie's eyes flutter open and suddenly widen with appall. She takes in a great gasp of horror becoming.

Lily heaves the jagged boulder and heaves it onto Cammie's head, burying it beneath the rock's weight. The rock teeters for a split second before tumbling over and falling beside her head. The face revealed is a messy, mushy gore. Cammie's glasses are cracked; a spider web fracture on the right lens and shards of the left lens spear inward, jutting her tender eyeball just below the pupil. The bridge of her nose is caved in and smashed upward. Cartilage impales her brain; the neurons are interrupted in their transmission. Her plump lower lip dons a deep gash; her two front teeth are collapsed inward toward a mouth where gums are pooling ruby puddles. Blood rushes in streams from her mouth, her nose, and from the indented abrasion on Cammie's forehead. Her corn silk hair is instantly streaked in red.

The girl on the ground is dead; their sacrifice has been made.

Lily takes in a deep breath of relief and peers up to Sabrina who retains her role in the deadly game.

"I am Cammie," Sabrina speaks.

"I don't like killing people," Lily states, a little shaken up.

"I am Cammie," her lover announces again.

"O.K., Sabrina, game's over. I can't believe that fat bitch bought in to all that bullshit about Possessor." Lily slightly giggles. "We have to get rid of her body."

"I am Cammie."

Lily hears Sabrina's claim again and realizes, with shock, that the voice is not that of her undead lover. The voice is different. It is pretty and sexy, kind of like the voice of those fat women on the other side of a sex line. *Oh my God*, Lily understands. *It is she. But how?* It was only a trick, like on the video. Possessor wasn't real; it never worked before! Lily cups her hand over her mouth and gawks at the body on the ground that is inevitably Sabrina. Shock envelops her being as her body begins to quaver uncontrollably.

Cammie hears her own voice emitting from the mouth of her new, eternal host and observes her hand. *Sabrina's hand*. The sacrifice for beauty; was it worth it? A tear forms in her new jade eyes as she notices her own body lying dead on the ground before her, horribly disfigured.

Confusions swarms through her head and she is beyond scared. The fear of everything rushes through her and she wants to hear a solacing voice to calm her, a voice of comfort. *Eric's voice*. Instead, the deafening, booming sounds drown her hearing. They are like loud voices of thunder. But they don't come from the clouds above her; they are erupting from the ground beneath her feet, from a world that waits to greet her.

Another tear.

A white dove rockets from the pine tree above her, soaring high to the heavens.

The Baths at the End of the Road

Corey strolled up to me half an hour after I had gotten home from the office. I was beneath the light of the scorching Arizona sun, watering the irises I had only planted three weeks previous. The stems of the plants were barely poking through the moist dirt.

"Have you seen *The Root*?" Corey asked.

My attention remained on the plants lined in a neat row. This had been my first attempt at gardening; a very relaxing hobby compared to the corporate politics of the advertising world. "Yeah, they're starting to come up," I answered as I gestured toward the plants with the tip of the water hose.

Corey laughed, and it didn't make a difference if he really meant it or not, his laugh was always fake. I suppose that was one of the qualities I had grown to love in my best friend who I had known for nine years. Not to mention, the way he fabricated most of what he'd witnessed in real life or heard on television. "Nah, I don't mean your posies."

"Funny," I remarked in monotone as I turned toward him. "Oh, you mean the roots of your hair. Yeah, better bleach them again."

Corey ran his fingers through his hair, trying to take notice of the fading bleach blond color at the tips. "You really think it looks bad? I was trying to grow it out to its natural color."

Corey's original hair color consisted of a beautiful chestnut hue. I'd always wondered why he had gone and bleached it. Of course, Corey kept up with all the gay trends. I mocked him. "Corey *au natural*? You mean you're going to be yourself for once? No more fake hair? Are you giving away your *Prada* collection too?"

"Fuck you," he chuckled in a way two best friends can only remark to each other in joking fashion. "Besides, I see your *Prada* collection is getting a bit of overuse these days." His hazel eyes made their way to my loafers.

"Touché." I pulled a cigarette from my breast pocket; I flipped and ignited my Zippo in one flowing movement.

"Anyway, I meant *The Root* as in the place itself. It's only right down the road from you."

Corey meant the bathhouse he had told me about after discovering it in a local gay magazine. According to the article written about it, the place had been in existence for over five years and a majority of the gay population in Phoenix hadn't a clue of its whereabouts. When Corey and I were doing our Monday night ritual of drinking down at a local gay pub known as *Kirmser's Too*, he had brought up the idea of the two of us going.

He always liked to do things like that; Corey was always on the cutting edge fads of the queer culture. I think part of that was because he was neglected by his parents since birth. His mother was an alcoholic and his father convinced him that being a homosexual meant an instant death sentence, not to mention a bullet ride straight to Hell. Nevertheless, he had moved from his parents' house at the age of sixteen and, once he had his freedom, went all out on collecting designer labels and mimicking every possible fad in the gay culture. He wanted to be one of the elite, the *A-Gays*. Between the after hours clubs and the threesomes, Corey had made his message clear. Still, as much as I despised that lifestyle of queer customs, I would always have a place for Corey in my heart. After all, he had been the first man to whom I had made love.

"Are you still on *that* kick? I thought bathhouses went out in the early eighties." I awaited a reply. Corey always had an answer for anything I said to him.

"They're making a comeback though. You have to come with me and try it out. There's a steam room, a weight room, and even a lounge that shows nothing but porn!" Corey was trying everything to sell me on the idea; although, he would never make a good salesman. Perhaps a crooked salesman.

"You've been there?" I was shocked that he knew as much as he did about the place. Of course, he could have gotten the information from the article. And there were always the many people who never believed Corey because of his habitual fabrications. For instance, he once tried explaining to a group of us that there was an underground sadomasochistic society known as the *Phoenix Strength Exchange* (or PSEX, as he had referred to its acronym). When we questioned him of its location, he claimed that, since he knew about it, he had to keep the location confidential. After a few weeks of hearing his accounts of men in underground caverns striking each other with leather tassels and suspending them in the air, our group got bored of hearing about it. Eventually, Corey's descriptions had faded away until he found something else with which to grab our attention.

"I've been there a couple of times," he claimed as his eyes shot behind me at the coming storm clouds.

I exhaled a stream of smoke and attempted to call his bluff. "What's it like?"

Corey bit at his lip for a moment. I was sure I had caught him in his own lie, but that was what was so fun about having a conversation with Corey. It was amusing to observe his gestures and how he squirmed his way out of lies like an escape artist. "Well...you walk around with nothing but a towel around your waist (some guys walk around naked) and it's like no holds barred. You can go back with a guy to their room, or even two or three guys if you want. Everything's dark, and the entire place is like one giant maze you can get lost in. A lot of the guys bring in poppers or head cleaner."

"Sounds dangerous," I commented as I flicked my cigarette onto the asphalt of the street.

"But that's what makes it so much fun!" Corey gave me one of his toothy grins; that was his version of puppy dog eyes. "They even supply you with free condoms!"

My stomach cringed for a moment; a sharp pain stabbed me from the side as if an invisible knife had sliced through my flesh and tapped my intestines. In the distance, the stroboscopic effect of lighting passing from one dark cloud to another told the story of a strong storm making its way to the city.

I snapped out of my unintentional slip into a daydream world. "Wow," I said with sarcastic enthusiasm accenting my voice, "free condoms! Now I have no choice but to go with you! Forget it."

"Donald," Corey whined. He was the only grown man I had ever known that could whimper like a spoiled child. "Pleeeeeeez."

"Forget it," I reiterated with authority that was spawn of the thunder. "What the hell do I need to go to a place like that for anyway? I'm a grown man, Corey, a mature, grown man who is very happy with his gay lifestyle. I outgrew the queer party scene a few years ago."

I sauntered to my front door and Corey followed right behind. He wouldn't let up; he was like a hungry puppy barking at my knees.

"You never go out with me anymore," Corey complained. "You always sit around here and do nothing but read books and water your plants. You don't even meet the guys at *Kimser's Too* anymore."

Being an advertising agent, I had learned how to negotiate. I've negotiated with the toughest clients on a weekly basis——haggling with numbers and percentages. But there always came a point when I would break. I gave in a lot to clients who showed me through their despairing gazes that they wanted to use my agency, yet they just couldn't afford such a high rate. The reality of life was not much different.

And Corey was right. I hadn't been hanging with the Boy-Toys anymore (that's what we called our close knit group). But, hell, it got old. Perhaps, once I turned thirty-two, I realized that life was no longer about partying everyday or finding the latest fuckable young model on the dance floor to take home. Maybe it was the beginning of losing all my friends. Nevertheless, I couldn't do that to Corey. I would always hold him near to my heart.

From behind me, Corey continued to beg. "C'mon, Donald. Do this for me. Please. I want to have a good time with you. We haven't done anything in ages."

I pivoted in my doorway and turned to face Corey. His lips were curled back and exposing that obnoxious grin of his. "OK," I gave in. "But if I get molested by some old priest, I'll never forgive you."

"WOO HOO," he yelled to the heavens.

"Never forgive you. You know that right?"

"Sure, right." His smile brightened; he reached out with his hand and tousled my hair.

Corey gave me directions to *The Root* and told me to meet him there at ten that evening. "Don't be fashionably late," he called back to me as he slipped behind the wheel of his Nissan Frontier. "You won't be wearing anything anyway."

I gently pushed my front door closed and a gust of wind fiercely blew it open. The day had gone from sunny to overcast. The trees were swaying in a ritualistic dance for the coming storm.

The generation before mine saw the bathhouse frenzy pop up all over America. I was only a young boy during the late Seventies and early Eighties, but as I grew into my gay self-realization, I couldn't help but want to know what the bathhouse craze was all about.

It seemed rather simple. Bathhouses were a way for any gay man from any walk of life to retain his anonymity of his sexual preference, and, at the same time, find other men just like him to engage in oral sex and sodomy. Of course, back in that time, which seemed an era away, many people didn't acknowledge the gay society as they do in this day and age. To be a queer was to be a freak. Nowadays, many people and businesses accepted the queer culture. It wasn't a matter of acceptance anymore; it was a matter of choice.

Until Corey had brought up *The Root*, I had thought that bathhouses no longer existed. I had thought they were places of gay legend and folklore. I had no clue that there was one located only five blocks down the road from where I lived. According to Corey's directions, *The Root* was located just before State Route 51, right before the underpass. He had explained that there was a red, flat metal sculpture on the North side of Indian School Road that signified the entrance to the parking lot. I was amazed at its location. "That's a business district," I remembered telling him. He shrugged his shoulders. I couldn't believe it; I had passed by that cluster of stucco buildings everyday and, never once, thought it to be the very location of a bathhouse. I supposed that it hid itself well behind its mask of professionalism that all of society had accepted.

As I exited the neighborhood known as the Idylwilde Historical District, I made a right onto Indian School Road. The asphalt shimmered like a pool of diamonds from the downpour of rain and oncoming headlights. It had been raining for the past hour and, according to the radio deejay, it was expected to last beyond midnight. My windshield wipers were set to 'high' and I glanced at the digital reading on the face of the radio that read 10:04. I was already late; after all, I had agreed to meet Corey at *The Root* at ten sharp. It didn't help the situation that the three traffic lights I encountered en route to the bathhouse signaled me with red as I hit each intersection.

Before I reached the underpass of State Route 51, I maneuvered my vehicle into the left lane. The radio volume was low. The sounds that echoed in the lonely silence of the vehicle were that of the incessant ticking of my turn signal and the large droplets of rain that made a metallic tap dance upon the roof of the vehicle.

I observed the buildings north of me, to my left, so that I might find the metal sculpture that marked *The Root*. The headlights of an oncoming vehicle illuminated the sculpture and, for a fleeting moment, I saw the contraption of metal geometric shapes shift back and forth, even fold and curve over one another in an abstract melt of twisted art. *Illusion of the mind*, I told myself.

After pulling into the entrance, I directed my car through the narrow alley and into, what appeared to be, a parking lot. I scanned the lot for Corey's *Frontier* and found it on the opposing side of the lot.

As I ejected from my car, I briskly made my way toward the brick-colored stucco building in a fleeting attempt to escape the downpour that had instantly dampened my clothes. I searched along either side of the building, looking for an entrance, finally coming upon a set of double doors tinted in black that gave off my wet reflection. It appeared as if tears were rolling down my entire body of my mirror image.

Pulling the door open, I was welcomed by a small twelve-foot-by-twelve-foot room. The walls were painted a Southwestern tan or red; it was hard telling considering how dark the room was. A door to the left included a miniscule peephole, a button that acted as a buzzer below it, and a computer printed sign encased in a plastic film that read, *Welcome to The Root! Please press the buzzer; we will be right with you.* I did as directed, though my finger trembled in the gesture. A sound filled the atmosphere like that of an old-fashioned telephone ring. It was followed by a high-pitched whir. and I heard a *click* as the door was automatically unlocked.

The room I walked into was isolated between the entrance and the bathhouse itself. There was another door that had to be *buzzed* open. However, the attendant that greeted me from behind a counter equipped with a hard plastic panel could only do this.

The attendant was an older man, probably in his fifties, with scraggly, mousy hair and an unkempt full beard. His belly hung over his jeans and was exposed through the opening of his leather vest. "Can I see your I.D.?" he asked in a husky voice.

I instantly pulled my driver's license from my wallet and pushed the card into the small metal compartment beneath the plastic partition that separated us. Just as quickly, he pushed the identification back.

"You want a locker or a room?"

"Can I smoke in here?" I had forgotten to have a cigarette on my way and the dainty atmosphere immediately put my nerves on edge.

"Smoking is allowed in rooms only," the attendant replied like a robot.

"I guess I'll take a room then. It's my first time here."

The man nodded as he hit the keys of a register. "Twenty-five dollars."

I handed over the money and, in return, he pushed a piece of paper beneath the panel. "Sign this," he ordered.

I grabbed the pen attached to the counter by a small chain and scrawled my signature. Pushing it back to the attendant I joked, "Does that mean I'm not a cop or something?"

"Correct," he replied. "Go on through the door." He pushed a button from his side and another high-pitched whir filled the air as the door unlocked.

Entering the next room, the attendant handed me a key and a white cotton towel. "You're Room 121," he announced.

"Any suggestions for a first time visitor?" I was eager to see what the guy's automatic responses would allow him to say to a question unwarranted.

"Yeah, try not to fall on your face." With that, he hoarsely cackled.

I proceeded to the first hallway I saw and it seemed endless. The hallway branched off into other halls; doors that announced the room numbers in stencil fashion made by black spray paint separated rooms on either side of the halls. Everything was barely lit by eclipsed lighting upon the ceiling. Music blared throughout the entire place, songs from bands like Erasure and the Pet Shop Boys.

The oncoming corner that greeted my walk held a mystery to it. *What was behind that corner*, I teased myself into fright. Of course, when I turned it, I found another lengthy corridor with others branching off of it. I continued to peer at the room numbers on the doors, searching for Room 121, and instantly felt lost. Corey was right; this place was like one giant labyrinth.

As I continued my search, I began witnessing men of all shades and sizes walking past me, clad in nothing but a bath towel wrapped around their waists. They all made the same gesture of rubbing their cocks beneath the towel as they pranced around. They were in search of a prey to satiate their hunger of sexual desire. Yet, none of them gave me a sideways glance. I realized that I was considered off limits. I was still in my street clothes, untouchable to the patrons of *The Root*. There was a feeling of safety in knowing this and, at the same time, a trepidation and anxiety of things to come. I began sweating profusely, perhaps intimidated by all the half-naked men passing me by. The entire ordeal caused me to search even harder for my room.

I spotted Room 119. The door to Room 120 was wide open. In the darkness, I observed a man lying flat on his stomach, his legs widespread and exposing his anus. Apparently, he was waiting for somebody to come in and start pulverizing him. Could it be that much more obvious?

I took a deep breath as I got to my room, fumbled with the key to get the door unlocked, slid into the darkness, and quickly shut the door behind me. As I flipped the light switch, I was disgusted by the size of the "room". It was no bigger than a jail cell. A small nightstand (with an ashtray, thank God) stood next to a bed. I don't even know if it could be called a bed; after all, it was half the size of a single and the mattress was made of foam covered by a thin white sheet. I could've gotten a full room down on Van Buren Street, in the heart of prostitute central for the same price. But, I reminded myself, I was doing this for Corey. I had to find him.

I lit up a cigarette and disrobed in between drags. After I wrapped the towel around my waist, I ran my fingers through my long locks of black hair so that they appeared somewhat styled. I observed myself in the mirror—my face had shadows cast upon it by the lighting, giving it a sharp-jawed look, and my flat stomach appeared better in the dim lit room than it did beneath the fluorescent lighting of my bathroom at home. Everybody looks better in less light. The bartender at *Kirmser's Too* deemed the illumination of the bar at the end of the night the "ugly lights." Fifteen minutes after last call, he would always announce, "OK guys, I'm turning on the ugly lights. Time to take a look at what you've been hitting on all night."

As I stubbed out my cigarette in the red, plastic ashtray provided by *The Root*, I heard the sound of the door to my room creaking open. I had forgotten to lock it. I turned my head quickly, catching a horrific glance in the mirror.

The reflection of what stood in the doorway was monstrous! It was that of a man with blue flesh and black lesions bursting all over his naked body. He had no eyes! There were only hollow sockets that oozed a thick creamy texture of blood from them. The man appeared dead and in the grave for weeks.

An uncontained yelp emerged from my throat as I jolted toward the undead man. However, once I confronted him, what stood in the doorway was simply a man. A man wrapped in a towel. His eyes were normal and his flesh was flecked with moles. That's it. He gave me a condescending and panicked look, as if I was a walking freakshow, and closed the door without saying a word. The anxiety was setting in. I had to get a grip on myself. I decided to roam the halls in search of Corey.

It didn't take me long to find him. After all, Corey was cruising every guy who came within proximity of him. Corey was a walking hard-on, and everybody that knew him was fully aware of that. It got me thinking of the guy back in Room 120, awaiting the anxious thrust of a stranger. Corey would do something like that. Although, I always convinced myself that, one day, he would grow up just as I had.

Corey made his way toward me, a shit-eating grin igniting his face. "I can't believe you made it!"

"I told you I would. I was a few minutes late; it's storming pretty badly."

"So," he paused, "what do you think?"

"It's kind of eerie," I admitted. "The guy in the room next to mine has his door opened and is lying naked on the bed."

"And...which room is yours?" Corey joked. "I'm just kidding man."

"So, what now?" I was unsure at what I was supposed to do. Was there a certain procedure or ritual that one had to do to be accepted in such a place?

"Go find yourself some men," Corey exclaimed as he eyed every person that walked by us. "Roam around; experiment a little. Live a little," he added.

"You're kidding." Then again, I had already known. The only reason to go to a bathhouse was to have sex. It wasn't like a bar; there was no alcohol, no good times in the sense of enjoying the company of your friends or an interesting guy you just met. There was sex and only sex.

"That's what I'm going to do," Corey said as he began to walk away from me and toward a handsome, tall stud whose eyes locked with his for but a moment.

"Where are you going?"

"To the steam room; you have to check it out." He giggled as he brushed past me and gave me a slap on the ass.

Steam room. Great.

I did as Corey suggested. I roamed the halls of *The Root*, witnessing a side of the gay culture I vowed to never again witness. It was so different from meeting a man in a gay bar or club. There were no introductions. All that was said in the voices that surrounded me was, 'Do you have a room?' or 'What do you like?' It was so easy to get laid in a place like this.

There were certain rooms that branched off the corridors and had leather drapes adorning the doorways. These rooms were coined "entertainment rooms." I had peaked inside a few of them, but refused to enter. One room contained a sofa and a big-screen television that showed the most gratuitous gay pornography I had ever seen. Men in that room stared at the television screen and stroked their cocks in rhythm with the action before them. Another room contained a suspended leather contraption that one could sit in with arms and legs spread eagle so that the general passerby could come in and fuck the superstar harnessed mid-air. In addition, a masturbating audience encircled the sexual event. There was another "entertainment room" comprised of an unending line of beds that had been pushed together. There were numerous men fucking each other while sucking others off. It was a festival of nudity and, to get a piece of the action, one only needed to disrobe from his towel and lie down on one of the beds. It wouldn't be long before the meld of flesh consumed one and pulled him into the sexual gratification. This room of orgies contained the pungent odor of sex sweat that permeated the air. It was awful, watching them all fuck one another and hearing their bestial grunts. The foul stench caused me to gag as I raced away from the doorway.

The Root was not the place for a guy like me; it was a building that housed kinky sex and horny homosexuals (some who were so repulsive that it was no wonder why they came to such a dainty place). I was beyond all of this or, perhaps, I had much more of an appreciation for life and a good self-esteem that kept me away from such places. Nevertheless, I wanted to leave as soon as possible. I had to let Corey know, and that meant having to track him down by finding the steam room.

I roamed the corridors with a hurried walk that sent a red flag to the rest of the patrons that I was nervous or scared. As I came to the end of one corridor, and about to turn into another, I saw a man following me from the corner of my eye. I broke off from the lengthy hall to an adjoining corridor. The man trailed my every step; not to mention, he sped up his walking pace to match my own. The idea began sending my mind in frenzy. Anything could happen in this place. People could get raped, or drugged, or even murdered and pulled off to one of the adjoining rooms to be found later. This was a place without boundaries.

I saw an opportunity to lose the man trailing me by ducking into one of the entertainment rooms. I made a fleeting entrance through the vertical, leather drapes and was welcomed by a dim red light.

Stall-like walls adorned the room I entered, creating a small maze within the room itself. I had to feel my way through the tangle of stalls, passing by others who had cupped my package or pinched my ass through the thin cotton of my towel.

I had come to a dead end. Three Formica walls, each with glory holes that came just below the waist, surrounded me. That is, these were holes that men could insert their cocks through in order to get sucked off without seeing the person doing it.

My adrenaline raced throughout my being and my stomach folded as I tried breathing as quietly as possible so that nobody would discover me. I stood against the back of one of the walls, staring at the open space before me where any man could enter. I was trapped; there was no way out, unless I crawled on my stomach beneath the stalls. I repositioned my stance and stepped in something cold and slimy. Men had sex in these stalls; men jacked off in these stalls. I knew what it was that I'd stepped into and was appalled.

Without warning, a stranger appeared before me. His cinnamon toned skin and dark hair told of his Hispanic origin. He had a tattoo of the sun upon his flat, firm stomach and the small rings that pierced his nipples and belly button fired back a brisk gleam from his position beneath the dim lighting. "How's it going?" he asked. His voice had a flowing sensuality to it, like that of a charming young man who holds your hand during a candlelight dinner.

"Fine," I replied as I cleared my dry throat.

With no pretense to the situation, he sauntered toward me and placed his hand under my towel, gripping my cock. He undid my towel, and it fell to my ankles as he got on his knees and began to suck. I put my head back against the stall and closed my eyes. His hands roved all about my buttocks, over my stomach, and over my chest. This man was beautiful and knew what he was doing; I could feel the strength in his hands as they roamed all over my flesh. My libido caused my mind to drift into a euphoric state. It felt good being with a man like this, with a stranger whose muscles were strong and sweaty with an aroma like that of sweet-smelling irises.

As he got to his feet, his towel had fallen to the ground. He pressed his body against mine and kissed me hard on the mouth. Our lips locked in unending passion and our tongues danced in each other's mouths. I cringed from the cold steel of his piercings that were forcefully pressed against my own naked stomach and chest. Our bodies rolled around in the stall. At first, he was up against me. Then, I had pushed him against one of the other walls and was performing the same actions he had done with me.

I felt a hand go for my buttocks. It felt about the curve and crept into the crack where two fingers glided into me. I rasped a breath of desire, of ecstasy never measured by any other sexual encounter I had experienced. The fingers moved in and out of me as I continued to kiss my Hispanic stranger. The scene became a dance of sexual rhythm—our bodies moving back and forth against each other, the fingers sliding in and out of me, our hardened cocks rubbing together and creating the feeling of crushed velvet upon silk.

I suddenly felt a sharp pain inside of my anus. It was like a tearing sensation, as if the probing digits were clawing their nails within my insides. "Ouch," I peeped with my lips pressed against those of the stranger. The agony flared up and sent a jolt to the rest of my body. I moved my buttocks forward, causing the fingers to exit, and pushed back the arms of the man I was kissing. However, his hands were at his side. I immediately opened my eyes and my heart almost stopped. Instead, *it* lurched forward with intense speed, causing the growing lump in my throat to cut off the oxygen to my lungs.

The Hispanic stranger before me had no eyes! Just as the reflection of the man I had seen earlier in my room, there were only two hollow sockets with a thick bloodlike substance grotesquely oozing from them. The man stood still, as if his corpse were frozen in place. He opened his mouth and a low continuous moan emitted from his throat. "Ahhhhhhhhhhhhh." As the horrible inflection relentlessly groaned, a swarm of beetles began spilling over his lips. The glistening blackness shot from his mouth and crept down his neck, trickling along his limbs as the beetles scurried about his body. I shot a quick glance behind me, where a withered hand with uneven purple fingernails was clawing at my ass through a glory hole.

I shrieked as I pushed past the Hispanic man turned dead. He turned around and extended his arm toward me, as if to keep me from leaving. Yet, he moved slowly; it was easy for me to escape his grasp given the panic that raced throughout my body.

I had to find Corey! I had to get the hell out of that place!

I sprinted through the corridors, racing past half naked men that stared at me in disgust. Making my way to a corridor to the right, I discovered an open bathroom. When I ran in, I instantly saw the frosted glass of the steam room. "Corey," I yelled with all my might. "Corey!"

The shadow of a figure came into view. Then, the shadow was against the glass door of the steam room; I could see Corey's bare ass pressed flat against the door. I yelled his name again before I ran to the glass door and pulled it open.

Steam roiled out of the room and seared my skin. The consumption of steam into my lungs caused me to cough. Corey pivoted toward me and smiled. However, before he had a chance to exit the steam room, a group of four other men came from behind and tugged on his arms and legs. To my horror, the four men were actually creatures like those that I had encountered. None of them had eyes, and they all bellowed in exasperating moans.

"Donald," Corey screamed. He reached his hand out toward me, but it was too late.

The creatures began clawing at Corey's torso with their rigid nails. Corey's chest split open as blood began racing down his stomach and into his crotch. His screams were far from over. Corey didn't stop screaming until two of the creatures' nails plunged into either side of his face and ripped at the skin. His flesh was pulled off and appeared to melt in their hands as the skin around Corey's eyes eerily sagged and drooped. The glass door shut closed. Corey's hand left a bloody imprint that became the last image I witnessed before bolting out of *The Root* with only my jeans on.

Images of that night haunt me every day that I am awake and every evening before I go to sleep. I still can't explain what it is I saw that night. Monsters? Undead creatures pretending to be human? Corey, my best friend, dying a terrifying death before my eyes.

I pass by that place on a daily basis—when I'm going to work, or the grocery store, or to pick up some take-out. Each time, I pray that the traffic light on that corner is green so that I don't have to stop my vehicle and turn to face that foundation of evil. Sometimes I wonder what infections are passed to others who enter that place. Why doesn't anybody *see* the patrons of *The Root* for what they truly are?

Last night, I heard a scraping sound against my living room window. I allowed it to continue as I tried to fall into a peaceful sleep. Eventually, I got up to investigate the noise. When I looked from the blinds of my window, I could've sworn I seen Corey. That is, Corey with no eyes. I chalked it up to a haunting memory of that unforgettable night; a traumatic scene etched into my mind that will always be with me.

This morning, when I walked out the front door, my garden of irises appeared to have been trampled upon. Had Corey come to visit me in the middle of the night, or was it a dream? What did they do to him? Is he dead? What's more, will he come back again? He knows that I will always hold a special place for him in my heart. Corey realizes that I live at the end of the road from the place he now calls home.

Trick of Fate

I. First Recorded Admission

I did it; I killed them all. Sure, I'll take credit for it; I sent their tortured and confused souls straight to Hell. Do I feel any remorse, any pity? Why? Does one feel remorse when he rids the world of a canine suffering from rabies? No, they do the dog a favor by blowing a fucking hole in its head. End the suffering, that's it; no need to contaminate the rest of the world with disease it would have spread. Just like *them*.

Did I mention I feel like a god every time I speak into this recorder? A god, yes! And I love to hear my voice, my dictation to an audience that will play this and all of the other micro-cassettes one day. I revel in the way my voice sounds when I'm playing the tapes back; I can always feel the emotion I'm trying to express with my voice. I hear the anger and the sarcasm when I put emphasis on certain words. And I envy the way I can speak into the recorder with an endless flow of diction. No long pauses; no loss for words. Probably better than the world's best storytellers, I'm sure.

Where was I? Oh, *them*. Yes, I lent them a hand out of *their* perplexing lifestyles and into peace. And one day, I know *they'll* be reborn and not have to be the way *they* were in this life. *I* am giving *them* a second chance, a door to go through so they won't spread their contagion to the rest of the populace. As if it's not bad enough already.

Some of them I strangled with my bare hands, some I repeatedly knifed with a hunting blade I've had since I was twelve, and some I simply blew a hole in their skulls as if they were mad dogs. I usually drive to the outskirts of Phoenix, where there is nothing except darkness and miles of desert, and I dump their bodies.

Always beautiful they are, handsome young men, many probably not old enough to purchase a beer at a bar. Ravishing men—these are guys that could make the big time modeling their bodies for the latest designer fad or make careers from starring in soap operas. Pretty boys. So goddamn pretty! Instead, they choose to stand on a street corner and sell their bodies for a couple twenties, and then spread disease to their next customer. They're reckless, courageous (I have to give them that much credit), and they won't hesitate to swallow some stranger's semen. Sick bastards!

I record everything, not just my venting and conquests to an invisible passenger that rides with me. I always make sure there is a new micro-cassette in the recorder before I pull up to my next target, and right when I roll down the passenger window (that sometimes gets stuck) I press the record and play buttons. When the tiny red light glows in the darkness of the vehicle is when I know it's all right to start talking to the street john who has already flocked to my car like a desperate fledgling.

I'll record the whole thing. From the negotiation of the price, to the repulsive sight of the hustler jacking himself off and moaning in self-gratification, to the act of me releasing their lost souls from this world. You see, I never touch them except when I'm attacking their bodies. I tell them that I want them to masturbate in front of me, that I'm a voyeur and I get off on watching young men jack off and swallowing their own cum. And, of course, they're so eager to make their money that they don't give the slightest hesitation acting out my false fantasy.

I played a tape the other day as I was folding my clothes. It was labeled Sean # 2. I had stabbed that young man more than thirty times. I lost count after twenty-nine; however, I heard a couple more plunges of the knife tear through his flesh before the tape ended. The sound a knife makes when it briskly enters and retreats from the flesh admittedly sounds like a metal shovel digging into a sandbox. The best part of the tape is when Sean screamed; the boy screamed like a girl and brought back the memory of my killing him. He screeched in horror, gasping for breath, as I plummeted the knife down again and again and, blessedly, again. His arms and legs flailed about the front of the car with strong reflexive movement. He cried as the deep wounds jutted out black blood all over his tight shirt, coloring it burgundy. Some specks of blood spattered near his eyes, and the tears he wept mixed with them and turned the streaks along his comely face into pink streams. I remember telling him it was going to hurt. It always hurts; but then it's so much better when it's over. I think Sean probably watches me from a netherworld now and wishes he could say thank you.

His brown eyes remained open and bulged with tears still dripping from them. Sometimes, *their* eyes stay open and sometimes *they* get one last breath in and use *their* diminished strength to push down *their* eyelids, to pretend it was a bad nightmare that *they* will go back to sleep from and awaken in the morning. I hate when *their* eyes are open, so I shut Sean's. Of course, I had to pull a latex glove from the back seat and put it on before I could touch the bloodied area. Sean was a good one though; he was a fighter. I'll miss that kid a lot. Sometimes it's sad to see *them* go, and I have to fight off slight bouts of guilt. But *they* have to go. *They* have created the Coming Plague, and *they* are the carriers of this disaster that only I can stop. Only I, yes! I have been chosen to be God of the Earth, to do His work.

I'm not quite sure how it had initially begun, only that it did. About eight years ago, when I was twenty-six, I went to this rave at some guy's house. I think his name was Helix or Felix, or some shit like that. Anyway, I remember he had practically everything on his body pierced. His right eyebrow was pierced twice, his nose, his nipples looked as if they had three rings in each of them (the guy was shirtless the whole time), and he even boasted about having his organ pierced. I couldn't imagine it! Having a ring go through your dick? That had to hurt! The guy immediately befriended me, although I was a little repulsed by the lack of hygiene for his body. I was very drunk; in fact, that was the last time I ever touched alcohol. I practically passed out in the bathroom, falling in and out of consciousness, and before I knew it, Felix had gained entrance to the locked door. When I opened my eyes, his cock was near my face, hard and rubbing against my cheek with the ring at the tip grazing my five o'clock shadow. I was so abhorred that I nearly puked the remaining alcohol left in my system.

I drove quickly, and ever so cautiously, back to my apartment. That night, I had nightmares of Felix and me. I had dreams of licking his organ and of him sodomizing me. I awoke in a dripping sweat, and my sheets were drenched. I immediately prayed. That's when *He* answered me. He said, "Terry, you are the one. You are the tool through which I must reach the world and strike out the evil."

I was elated. Thus, in eight years, with the help of His strength, I have stricken down over seventeen of *them*. I never get caught because the authorities know it has to be done. And they know I can't be stopped. I don't even know if there exists a force strong enough to bring me down.

I'm pulling the car to a halt so I can load in another micro-cassette. I've been driving around this area the last couple months. Here is a stretch of bad area, between Sixteenth and Fortieth Streets on Van Buren Road. If you drive west to Central Avenue, not really that far, Corporate Phoenix engulfs everything around you. Glass and steel buildings tower above you like antennas to another world. Men in three piece Armani suits with their satchels and cell phones. Versace wearing pretty boys who have afternoon coffee dates at the Plantation. Hell, half those guys in their Eclipses and BMW's are customers that come to this area on a weekly basis.

I better stop this thing and put in another cassette before the tape ends. My next victim is only a hundred yards away.

II. Tricks

Rick stands back from the corner of Twenty-Eighth Street and Van Buren, back in the shadow of a towering two-story building that was once a bar with a residence above it. Now it is condemned with plywood stretched over the doorway and bars shielding entrance through broken windows. He leans against the red brick building, near graffiti that sports a local gang's insignia in white spray paint. When he balances himself away from the condemned building, Rick slings his white t-shirt over his left shoulder and adjusts his cock from the uncomfortable position to which it conformed in his skin-hugging Levi's. He sucks in his stomach so that it reveals a flat boyish figure and observes Ronnie who stands at the edge of the curb and stares down traffic with his strutting eyes. It's as if Ronnie's eyes are facing off with the headlights of the many cars that stop and go at the busy intersection. It's especially busy for a Friday night.

It is Ronnie's second night hustling, and Rick observes this in the new kid's sloppy technique. Ronnie is trying too hard—walking twelve feet west, pivoting with his ass first, and then strutting in the opposite direction. He has the right attitude but needs to work on his body. Ronnie is thin like the heroin addicts that shoot up down the end of the alley off Thirty-Second Street. His scraggly, blond hair is in an oily, disheveled mess.

The clientele consists of doctors, lawyers, perverts, and even police officers that want a pretty-faced young man to suck their cocks and then shove the john back to the street curb. If Ronnie is going to survive, he needs to show the clientele that he's in control of everything including his looks, the negotiation, and the hustle.

The boy waves down cars with his hand; he's too eager to get a date.

Rick recalls telling Ronnie that you never wave down the cars! The people that drive through this area will know who you are and what you are about. If they want a date, they'll ease their cars to the side of the curb and roll down their window to negotiate. A good trick will not have to approach their customers; a good trick waits for the customers to approach him.

Rick has been hustling the streets of Phoenix for the past year, ever since he left his parents place because he couldn't put up with their shit anymore. Rick lived with his parents until he was twenty-two; he just couldn't hold down a job long enough to get the money to move into his own place. What, with first and last month's rent, along with a sizable security deposit, it was going to cost him at least fifteen hundred bucks to get his own apartment. He was tired of his father's alcoholism, his constant ordering of Mother around, and their fights that would last until four in the morning. Late enough for Rick to not get sleep and arrive late to work all the time. So he left.

His first trick made him a bit queasy. He had never tasted another man's semen, and wasn't expecting the bitter tang that shot into his mouth and crawled down the back of his throat. Soon he learned that it wasn't always that way and that the client's weren't always dirty and ugly men. He realized the wide range of the clientele that picked up the local johns: rich guys, married guys, and professional men with good looks. They never wanted the same thing. Of course, they all wanted to get their rocks off, but some of them wanted to be held, some wanted a simple hand job while being talked dirty to, and Rick met a guy once who took him to a cheap motel down the street and danced with him for an hour. Just the two of them, holding on to each other and making small steps left and right.

Rick's good looks make him a better date than the other johns— wavy brown hair, picture perfect face, and a defined body that isn't too buff to retain a boyish, angelic figure. Three quarters of the other johns are strung out all the time, and it shows in their tired faces. The streets age youth; there is no scientific creation to date that can transform a nineteen year old into the trite-looking body and mentality of a forty year old.

Rick is one of the older johns, and he has seen dozens of hustlers come and go. Sometimes, where they go, he doesn't know. Only that they try it out for a couple of days and come to their senses. They probably run back home. He tries to befriend the new boys; tries to teach them how to be safe and how to stay in control. This is a very dangerous business and if you slip once, you could be dead just as quickly as you ran up to that first car, that first date.

Rick wants to get out of the business but doesn't have enough money yet. He usually gets together with some of the other guys at the end of a night's work and they split the cost of a hotel room. Usually there are five guys in the same room that sleep through the day and check out in the evening to start over again.

For a while, Rick discovered the pleasures of crystal meth. He felt like a saint when he pushed the substance up his nose, and had energy like never before. After months, Rick realized that he was always out of money; it all went to the meth! His body was getting sickly thin, and he wondered how long he could live like that.

He's been off the drug for a few months now, and has stashed six hundred dollars in his boots that he will use to leave the business. Get that apartment, his own place, get a real job, and maybe go on real dates and meet people that will be in his life longer than one night. *Soon. One day very soon*, he's been telling himself lately.

"Rick," Ronnie yells back at him. The lanky kid is walking toward the building where Rick watches from the darkness that looms over him. "I can't get a date, man."

"I told you," Rick explains, "you're trying too hard."

The protégé casts his eyes downward, discouraged.

"It's only your second day. Don't walk up and down the street like you're a prostitute on Hollywood Boulevard. Are you sure you want to do this?"

Ronnie glares up at Rick. "I have to make money, man!"

"OK, take off your shirt and toss it over your shoulder. Like the way I have mine."

"Why?"

"Don't ask why; just do it. It's kind of like a flag johns give to let the people know they're available."

"Like a 'vacancy' sign, right?"

Rick laughs harder than he has in the last six months; he hasn't laughed this much since the ordeal with Gabe. "You're a riot," Rick chuckles wildly.

"Now what?" Ronnie continues his asking of advice as he glances at the missed opportunities that speed down the road behind.

Rick pulls out a small, fine-tooth comb and hands it to Ronnie. "Run this through your hair. Comb your hair back and keep it behind your ears."

Ronnie does this without question and hands the comb back.

"Now, just walk out to the curb and stand there looking at the drivers that pass by. Don't wave them down! I told you that once already, and you're still doing it."

"Well, how the hell else am I suppose to stop them?"

"You don't wave your hands! Just stand there. If they're interested, they'll pull alongside the curb. And don't run to their car like you're desperate! If you do that, then you're fucked with negotiating a price. Understand?"

"Yeah," Ronnie says, more sure of himself.

"Now go," Rick yells humorously as he pushes Ronnie off and slaps his ass in a friendly manner. "Go, Ronnie, go," he cheers.

Ronnie's a good kid, and Rick wonders what he's doing out here. He reminds Rick so much of Gabe. Rick still holds guilt for what happened that night six months ago.

Rick observes Ronnie, and the kid appears to be taking his advice. *Gabe*, Rick recalls, and he makes a mental note to himself. *Keep this kid from making any wrong moves. Save this one.*

III. Cassette Two

The only time I allow a pause on a tape is when I am beginning a new one. I have to be positive that the black thread of the micro-cassette reels two full turns so that I know, without a doubt, that a single word is not missed on the recording. I tend to think of my words as art, as the pieces that fit together into a gigantic canvas of salvation. Perhaps, the world will come to know it as an audio version of a second Bible. Therefore, I must be absolute that not a shred of diction is omitted.

Everything is shrouded in darkness where the car parks, silently running, purring like a cat, a panther on the prowl. There are no streetlights flooding the car in a dreadful spotlight, and I have the headlamps turned off so that the only light is that of the miniscule red dot from the recorder.

I'm watching the boy on the corner of Twenty-Eighth and Van Buren. I can't help but notice how he seems different from the other young men I've picked up before. He appears fidgety, false, and it's obvious that he's new at *their* game. Oddly enough, I think he's consorting with another person somewhere behind him but it's hard to tell, considering how dark it is over there. I wonder if he's a plant? Perhaps a cop ready to arrest the next person that he climbs into the car with. That would justify his communicating with an unknown figure that's evidently hiding out. He's disappeared now, strutting his jean-hugging ass near the entrance of the old Broiler Room Bar. I wonder...no, it wouldn't make sense. Besides, the police won't arrest me. They'll see I'm doing them a favor; I'm making their jobs a little bit easier. And if they try, well, I'm invincible, invisible. A panther.

Just my luck, another obstacle. Perhaps the devil is attempting to protect his minions. The red letters below the unlit speedometer spell out the warning "check alt" with a small, electric red picture of a rectangle encasing a plus and minus sign. I remember a friend I had in college telling me that if your alternator is about to go out, keep the vehicle running. Once you turn off the car, it will not start again until you install a new alternator. So I will keep the car running. It doesn't matter much because I do all of my work in my car. I'll grab the kid, kill him, dispose of the body outside the city, and take the car back home. I'll worry about the car tomorrow; there are more important things to do tonight.

The boy has returned and is now stripped of his shirt that drapes over his shoulder, just like the rest of *them* do. Instead of traipsing back and forth on the sidewalk, as he was doing just ten minutes ago, he simply stands there. His stillness is like that of a statue, as if he is to be admired by the passerby. The boy has no chest; I can practically see his ribs peeking through his flesh as if he were starving. He's very weak and I don't think he'll put up much of a struggle. He will be an easy one, oh yes! I feel giddy. There is a tickling sensation in my stomach! My cock is hard, and I want to unzip my Dockers and masturbate, but I know I won't feel as excited when I kill the young man that awaits me.

I just turned on the headlamps but they don't seem as bright. I'm turning the knob of the erected gadget that controls the lamps so that the dome light will come on. It seems that the inside of the car is lit in a weak glow. Damn alternator!

There is no time. I'm placing the gearshift into "Drive" and am easing my way to Twenty-Eighth. The young man that stands there is so lovely.

IV. Fate

Rick surveys Ronnie, as the kid obeys the instruction to which he was offered. *That's much better*, Rick thinks as he notices a sedan approaching. The car is moving cautiously along the asphalt as other cars are racing by. One honks at the driver who is obviously moving too slowly. The headlights of the advancing vehicle are dim and only half the intensity than that of the other vehicles that endlessly dash down Van Buren Road.

Rick forcefully shrugs his shoulders to rid the sensation crawling up his back and around his sides to where his heart begins to abnormally race. The chill is unexpected and the scene seems all too familiar. He cannot place the recognizable panorama, but knows, deep within his knowledge, that it has happened before and, maybe, before that. Although he knows not what meaning the image has, this scene replayed, his mind attunes to the dimming headlights. Those headlights, how they bring back a memory. Déjà vu? Perhaps. Of Gabe? Even more. Rick's hands quaver like a thumbed coil spring as his face becomes pasty by a haunting sweat. What is it about those headlights that faintly glower as if the life of them is slowly diminishing? Death. Gabe.

Rick glares with intense eyes, like a protective eagle perched at its nest, as the beige sedan eases to the curbside. He sees Ronnie casually stride to the vehicle as the passenger window goes down three fourths of the way. In the shadowy quarters of the sedan, Rick makes out the face of a man that looks a bit older than he does. His face is sharp as a hatchet and the flesh hugs the man's skull in youthful grace. Rick studies the driver's mouth move; his head is bowed down with eyes that cast upward. The man's expression is insidious looking, slightly crazed or perhaps in need of a fix. Meanwhile, Ronnie's head and arms are resting on the bulk of window as he converses with the driver, gesturing with his hands the numbers three then two.

It's as if a gleaming flash envelops Rick's sight of the negotiation for a brief moment, and then he sees a different scene...

...The scene is familiar to him; it is the mistake that preoccupies his thinking on a daily basis. He sees Gabe, or the memory of Gabe. Young Hispanic, androgynous Gabe with his high cheeks and thick eyebrows. Gabe's hair is long and almost reaches his shoulders in a serene wave of black silk. Where the beige sedan is currently idling is, instead, an old, dented pick-up truck with primer as dull as dead eyes. Gabe is pushing the button of the pick-up's door and pulling on the handle to climb into the truck. Rick wants to run away from his circle of friends and to the truck driven by an eccentric man who has caught his attention. He wants to bolt to the truck and keep Gabe from shutting the door and sealing his fate. *No! Stop him before it's too late!* Instead, Rick stares in awe, reassuring his anxieties with the flash-forward that he will see Gabe's camera perfect smile in another hour or less. However, Rick has such a fanatical protectiveness for the kid's safety. He watches the truck make a u-turn as the headlights temporarily blind him. Then, all that is left, are the blood red taillights that get smaller as the vehicle proceeds further down the road.

Gabe never returned. A week and a half later, Rick gazed in terror as the local police pulled the young man's gutted body from a back alley dumpster. He wanted to imagine that flawless smile on Gabe's face, that innocent perfect grin, but instead was subject to lips that curled in a horrified pause, an illustration of dread stained in the powder blue foundation of Gabe's dead visage.

Rick blamed himself for Gabe's death. He should have followed his instinct and taken the trick before Gabe did. After all, Rick knew he would have had a better chance fighting off the perpetrator. Not Gabe, no. He was so frail and couldn't fend for himself. He couldn't even fight off some of the other johns that wanted to ruin his cute looks because they were envious.

Gabe had only been hustling for a week before he was murdered. Rick befriended him on the first day the boy strolled down Van Buren. In fact, Rick was the first person Gabe to which he spoke and confided his fears. Rick instantly fell in love with Gabe, loved Gabe yes, and thought the young man was too intelligent to be wasting his life on the streets. Gabe had a charm that attracted Rick, perhaps those hazel eyes that couldn't be intimidated by his own. And the talks they had in the motel rooms went on for hours, keeping them from sleep. They'd talk straight into the afternoon hours while the rest of Corporate Phoenix went to work. Sometimes their discussions were of their families, sometimes their passions, and, other times, of their future.

Rick wanted Gabe, and he knew this from the moment he met the comely young man. He was only two years younger than Rick and Rick was picturing a time when he and Gabe could share an apartment in Central Phoenix and become lovers. The delighted sensation that filled Rick's body when Gabe was spending time with him plunged Rick into the realms of love for the first time. Rick had grown to love Gabe, and had never known love before. He had never known the staring into another's eyes with such intensity, or the rush that tore through one's body upon meeting up with the one for whom they cared. Rick had never experienced jealousy, and to know that Gabe may be on a date with a stranger made him insecure and often hurt. He wanted to take Gabe out of this dirty business, make love to him, and spend many years together talking, reveling in each other's lusting gazes, and making love in their own plush bed. But it would never happen.

No, Gabe was dead. Dead, and it was probably his own fault! He would not let this happen again. Not again, no!

Snapping out of his reverie, Rick sees Ronnie grasping at the handle of the sedan where the man with the menacing smile awaits to drive off with him. Instinct. Once again, that same instinct! But this time, Rick won't let this feeling of uncertainty go. The sensation that fills in his stomach is like that of an internal voice telling him that it is he who must take this trick and there need be no other reason. He couldn't save Gabe, but he will make sure that Ronnie doesn't meet up with the same fate. And if he's completely wrong about the guy negotiating with Ronnie, if it all turns out to be a paranoid fascination produced by his guilt for what happened to Gabe, so be it.

Rick grabs the t-shirt from his shoulder and jogs up to the car before Ronnie takes his place into the passenger seat. He pops his head into the door that is still ajar, says, "Excuse us a moment," and grabs Ronnie by the forearm, pulling him from the clutches of the car and the driver. The man reaches to pull the door shut, and the dome light slowly fades as if it is running off very little electrical juice.

"You better hope he doesn't take off!" Ronnie scorns.

"So what if he does?" Rick counterattacks.

"He's the first date I've had in two nights, man."

"I can't explain myself, but you have to let me take this trick."

Ronnie laughs as if he's out of his mind. "You're kidding, right. You've been out here a year, man; you can get any trick that you want."

"Please," Rick begs, "please let me take this one."

"He's offered me two hundred dollars! I need the money, man"

"OK, if you let me take him, I'll give you half."

"I don't see what the big deal is."

"Fine. I'll give you all the money. I promise...I'll give it all to you if you let me take this trick."

"Are you crazy, man?" Ronnie quickly mulls the offer over in head. "OK, but you better not be messing with me."

A smile of content fills Rick's face as Ronnie cranes his neck back to the car that continues to idle at the curb. "I'm not messing with you."

"Promise, right? Promise you'll give me the full two hundred."

Ronnie reminds Rick of a defenseless dog that has been kicked. "Promise."

Rick gives Ronnie a passing hug and approaches the vehicle. He climbs into the car and forcefully shuts the door, turning to his date.

The man turns his head to look through his windshield. He notices Ronnie walking away from the car. "Where's Ronnie going?" the man asks with concern that knits his eyebrows.

"Ronnie's not feeling well. My name's Rick. Ronnie told me you offered him two hundred, so I wouldn't expect anything less."

"Are you as good as Ronnie?"

"Better. Anything goes, no holds barred."

"All right, that sounds like what I'm looking for," the man cackles as he pulls the gear and drops it down to 'Drive'.

They continue to drive east on Van Buren; the buildings that are nothing but ruins and old warehouses become sparse. They cross the threshold out of the john district and make a turn on Forty-Fourth, where the driver directs the car north to Indian School Road. Rick observes the closed businesses they drive by which, at this point, consist of bars that have emptied their clientele, office suites, and strip malls. All the lights are green for the driver and the street names go by in a flash. McDowell Road...Oak Street...Thomas Road, where a large rectangular bank sits on one side and the Arcadia Crossings shopping center fills up half a city block on the other side of the road. Then Osborn Road, where the little businesses and apartment complexes densely line the road. Finally, Indian School Road, where the driver makes a right and proceeds east again. There is an odd silence in the vehicle. No talking, just the hurried breathing of the driver as if he is overly enlivened by Rick or is having an asthma attack.

"Are you OK, guy?" Rick asks.

"I'm fine Rick," the driver responds. He doesn't bother to direct his attention to Rick. Instead, he continues to focus on the lighted asphalt with the yellow turn lane and the dotted white lines of the four-lane road.

"You got a name?" Rick asks as he adjusts his body more comfortably in the vinyl seat that sticks to his sweating back.

"Yes, of course, how rude of me. I'm Terry. I would shake your hand but I very well can't drive while doing that, now could I?"

Rick takes his hand and places it on Terry's knee. He begins feeling Terry up toward his crotch. The driver stubbornly jerks his leg and the car briskly slows as Terry's foot yanks from the gas pedal. Rick retreats as Terry says, "Will you just let me drive. Don't touch me while I'm driving!" There is a scorn to his voice, a raise in his octave, which Rick chalks up to anger and fright. It is apparent that the man doesn't want to be handled; it's as if Rick's touch risks the man named Terry to the plague.

Rick remains quiet, as he calculates what it is that Terry wants. A lump begins to swell in Rick's throat; his palms become infused with cold sweat, and his mind pursues a way out of a possible impending danger.

Soon, Terry and Rick are out of the Phoenix city limits and in Scottsdale, where the wealthy dine on fifty-dollar dinners and inhabit houses that are larger than the businesses that permeate south Phoenix. The car turns north, onto Scottsdale Road, and then veers east onto Shea Boulevard.

An hour has passed since Rick first stepped foot into the car and, with each passing minute, he becomes more impatient, more scared. However, he tells himself to keep in control. "If you can't find the motel you're looking for, you can always pull the car into an alley and we could do it there."

"Don't get too restless, Rick. We're almost there. You have to understand that I'm a very private guy and I can't chance any of the public or the police to catch me paying money to a young man as yourself for sexual favors."

Rick understands; perhaps that does make a bit of sense. But, hell, all the way out here? Something isn't right, and this Rick knows.

Terry begins speaking again, and the houses on either side of Shea Boulevard fade as darkness begins swallowing the road. "I want you to know that I'm not one of you."

"One of..." Rick says, baffled.

"A queer. A guy that has sex with other guys."

Rick laughs a tired laugh, for he's heard that line before. "Well, guess what, Terry? You picked up another guy."

"Why do you do it?" Terry inquires.

"Let's see, I have sex with guys because I like guys. I can't help how I feel Terry; the woman's body simply doesn't do it for me. I have sex with guys for money because it's a good way to make a lot of money quickly. I don't plan on doing this the rest of my life, you know. I have goals and dreams like everybody else."

"Do you ever fear getting diseases? Don't you feel guilty about passing them on to other people?"

"First off, Terry—if that *is* your name—disease is everywhere. You don't have to get it from fucking another guy. Disease is all around us and you can't stop it when it's your time. It's fated. You ask if I feel guilty passing it to other people? Well, for your info, I'm a very safe guy and I take all the appropriate measures." Rick reaches his hand into his right pocket, pulls out a handful of Trojan condoms, and tosses them on the adjoining vinyl seat.

Terry looks from the road to the condoms in a sneer of disgust. A frown of revulsion curls his lips and causes him to clench his teeth.

"Look, if you don't want to do this you shouldn't have picked—" Rick's sentence is interrupted by the site of the dim tarmac before them. The headlights barely light up the road and streetlights are virtually absent this far out, almost to the Indian reservation. There are hardly any buildings out this far; nothing save for the two-lane, rough asphalt and the surrounding desert. "What's wrong with your lights?" *Dimming headlights.*

"It's the alternator, Rick. The alternator is going out, see?" Terry points to the idiot light on the console that emits a brilliant red brighter than the headlights.

Rick's hands begin to tremble. *What is wrong with this guy?* "You have to turn the car around," he demands. "You can't go any further Terry, or we'll both be stuck out in the middle of nowhere."

"Don't fret," Terry says, "we're stopping now." The driver eases the car off the side of the road, where the tarmac leads to dirt.

"Wait!" Rick anticipates. "Don't shut off the engine."

"I said don't worry! I know what I'm doing. I'll let the engine idle while you do your thing and then we'll turn back." There is a smile on Terry's face. Lips barely upturned. A false smile.

Rick considers opening the passenger door and lunging out of the vehicle, but there is no place to go out there. There is nowhere to run but the desert; no refuge save for the towering saguaro cacti with their long, prickly arms and a stretch of never-ending dirt and rock. *No safety out here, no. Maybe Terry is just a pervert,* Rick rationalizes, *give him what he wants and let him drive back close enough to the city so that you can jump out of the car at the first traffic light.*

"Give me the money first," Rick insists.

"Well, all right." Terry thumbs through his leather wallet, pulls out four fifties, and hands them to Rick. Terry makes sure that he holds on to the very edges of the bills so that Rick's fingers don't graze his.

Rick stuffs the money where the condoms once were. "So, do you want me to blow you?"

"Oh, that won't be necessary. I'm more of the voyeur type. Take the jeans off, Rick. Let me see you."

Rick peels off his pants. His cock is limp; however, Terry is pleased with its size.

Terry continues with his fantasy and checks the floorboard to make sure the red eye of the recorder is staring back at him. "I want you to masturbate; I want you to cum all over yourself and swallow your own semen."

For two hundred, Rick thinks, *this is too easy.* He's had worse requests than this. The uneasiness in his stomach begins to subside. The guy is definitely just a pervert. Rick can usually prolong his orgasm, but will hurry for this guy. Hurry so he can get back home; get back to Ronnie and the guilt of Gabe that got him here in the first place. Gabe, yes! For the love of Gabe and for the safety of Ronnie. And there need not be any other reason, but that it was his instinct to take this trick. It was his calling. Sometimes, reason cannot be justified; perhaps it is simply fate.

Rick handles his cock with his left hand and cups his testicles in his right, making sure to pull them close to the base of his hardening organ so that he will ejaculate sooner. He pulls up his hand and spits into the palm, using the saliva as a lubricant for his stroking. Up and down the length of the solid shaft, his hand slides in slippery caresses. He spreads his legs as far apart as the confined passenger side of the car will allow, so that he can feel the tingling of his prostate. Rick closes his eyes and tilts his head back as a soft moan escapes his mouth.

Terry studies the boy with heated breathing and licks his dry lips. His own cock is hard, and he wants to moan with the boy. Excited, he rubs his hand against his own organ that begs for attention and is under the thin lair of cotton fabric. *It feels so good*, he thinks, and mouths, "Ohhh."

The groan coming from Terry seizes Rick's attention as he opens and eye to glance over at the man who is also masturbating with his khaki's on. A slight smile graces Rick's face, an elation of doing a job well done, of doing what he does best. He continues to stroke himself, feeling closer to climax.

Terry is now handling the bulge that is outlined by his pants. He keeps a keen eye on Rick's own masturbating and watches the tip of the young man's penis, waiting for the eruption of milky silk. He clenches to his cock harder, trying to keep his moans silent. *Nothing can stop me*, he reasons, *not even this temptation!* Before he can use his will power to stop his autoerotic gesture, Terry feels his cock spurt out semen into his briefs with a number of short, convulsing shots. He can feel the smooth, creamy texture seep under his testicles in warm trickles. He is moaning, then practically crying, as he grasps alongside his seat for the sharp hunting knife that is wedged between his door and the floorboard. His grip furiously tightens onto the hard rubber handle as he analyzes Rick's climax.

Rick feels he is about to explode and opens his eyes to view it. One, two, than a third long stroke down the entire length of his pulsing cock as the relieving tingle in his prostate reaches its peak. At the same time, a thick stream of semen discharges into the air and splats down onto Rick's carved chest. At the exact time the pheromones in his brain release the pleasure of ecstasy, he witnesses a gleaming from the corner of his eye. His heart jolts into immediate alarm. *What was that, a knife? For Gabe. For Ronnie. Dimming headlights.*

Rick hurries to his senses as semen trickles alongside his chest, down to his stomach, and into the matted hairs that surround the base of his cock.

"Swallow your semen, Rick. Taste your own killer," Terry casually says with a slight smirk. Terry grips the knife tighter and feels his knuckles ache from the excessive clutching.

Rick's mind sprints for an escape, for a way to stop the lunatic beside him who is concealing a knife. Rick knows it's a knife.

"Well, I'm waiting," Terry impatiently states.

Rick cups his hand and runs it up his stomach and chest to collect the semen that slowly moves in thick streams. His gaze meets Terry's and, instead of putting his cupped palm to his mouth, Rick pushes it over into Terry's face and rubs it all about. "You sick fuck," Rick yells as he immediately turns to pull the handle of the door open. There is a click. The door budges slightly before Rick notices that the lock is in a down position. He pulls it up while searching behind him. Terry is flailing all about, trying to wipe the stinging cum from his eyes with one hand and wielding a seven-inch blade in the other.

Rick pushes the car door open, falls halfway from the vehicle, and then feels a sharp, cold sting penetrate his back and tear at his insides. The pain is so overwhelming that Rick can't feel his legs. It's as if they've gone numb. The sound of a soft, hollow swish invades his mind, and then he can feel oozing warmth flooding his back. When he looks down to his stomach, he sees nothing but crimson trails of blood.

He is tugged back into the vehicle and turned onto his back, where the stinging is greater than any other pain experienced. Rick sees the face of Terry, slimy with jism and contorted with such vehemence that changes the man's features. His eyes are squinted in rage, his clenched teeth showing through parted lips, and his cheeks are bulged. Then come the hands that wrap tightly around Rick's neck. Rick's arms and legs flail about. One of his legs kicks the headlights on, which creates no light whatsoever in the deserted area. He doesn't have the strength to fight back, no; the flaring pain in his back subsides all his vigor.

Tighter, he feels Terry's grip; tighter, and there is no more oxygen in his lungs. Rick can feel the blood in his face pulsing and the warmth it brings. No air, and Rick clenches his fingers at anything above him, missing Terry completely. Dimming. Fading. The last thing Rick remembers is his naked body hitting the dirt and rolling a couple of times along the small pebbles and bits of broken glass of the desert floor.

Terry rushes back to the car and feverishly wipes his hands on his clothes. He quickly slams the door and throws down the gearshift as he speeds onto the road, tires horrifically screeching into the silent night. Darkness is all around him. It is a blackness that can swallow up anything; for the inky world is infinite and everywhere. Terry tries to turn on the headlights when he realizes that they are already on. There is no more juice from the battery to keep them lighted. Terry can see nothing—no sparkle from a bit of light and no fluorescent colored lines to mark the tarmac. He squints his eyes as much as possible to make out the road, but cannot view a thing but the dark night. Before he gets a chance to slow down and figure the scenario through, the tires of the vehicle grip the rough edge of the road and the sedan fiercely swerves off the asphalt.

The ride is suddenly rough, and Terry tries to brake when he abruptly hits a boulder that flips his car twice across the road to the other side. He is in utter shock and awesome pain. Terry is upside-down in the car, and there is something blocking his breathing. He shudders as he hears the sound of an appalling gurgle as he takes in a breath. The hunting knife is lodged in the man's throat. The last thing Terry sees is the red eye of the recorder. The last thing he imagines is that nothing can stop him. The last thing Terry hears is the click of the recorder as it comes to an end.

V. Loop

…Rick stands back from the corner of Twenty-Eighth Street and Van Buren…
…Rick forcefully shrugs his shoulders to rid the sensation crawling up his back…
… The headlights of the advancing vehicle are dim and only half the intensity than that of the other vehicles that endlessly dash down Van Buren Road.…
…The chill is unexpected and the scene seems all too familiar…

...And can it be that fate is strong enough to continuously loop time and space to balance good and evil? The force of fate allows Rick to jump into the madman's car who calls himself Terry, to keep Terry from killing, so that negative does not overpower the positive in the world. It is fated so everything may continue to remain in balance. There must be both good and evil; it is inevitable. In this world, in this universe within other universes, Rick is the positive overwhelmed by a guilt that kept him from saving before and Terry is the monster who cannot be stopped.

…He cannot place the recognizable panorama, but knows deep within his knowledge that it has happened before and, maybe, before that…

...Rick gives Ronnie a passing hug and approaches the vehicle. He climbs into the car and forcefully shuts the door, turning to his date...

Circles...
Circles...
And circles again.

Joseph's Request

He used to watch me. It was so unlike him just to study me like a voyeur, like a jealous love watching his sexual partner rub bodies with a dance-floor lust. From the corner of my bedroom, next to the freestanding, vertical mirror, his sapphire eyes pierced me and observed every move, heated stroke, and blissful orgasm.

That is what I usually noticed when I caught his presence from the corner of my eye, when I directed my attention from the current lover sucking me off or fucking me deep and hard—slight outline of his transparent, robust form and crystalline eyes that veritably glowed in the darkness of the bedroom. Those azure eyes beamed through me and saw what was happening inside of me, with every lover's final, salty thrust. It was those eyes that burned for me the way they had back in the day when he'd fucked me. Oh, I recall that gaze, that biting squint of his eyes! I remember how they focused on my hardened chest, studying the sweat of pain and pleasure that ran between the deep crevice between my pectorals as he released himself within me.

Before last night, Joseph had never budged, nor had he advanced toward me. In fact, he never made any such gesture, save for the times that his spectral figure catapulted upward and hovered near the ceiling to glance down at me (that usually occurred when I was about to cum). As I would reach my climax, the bastard would leisurely rise above me like a balloon full of helium. And in that lazy movement toward the heavens, he would inspect me as if he were taking mental notes of the elated expression on my face. His own face, the strong jawline and the low brow, would remain unscathed by emotion. Plain and simply: straight-faced. Studying.

It was wild, his unemotional gaze! It sent a rush of adrenaline that pulverized my entire being as my current lover forcefully ejaculated inside of me and my semen oozed down either side of my stomach. At the same time, it was intensely eerie. That, in turn, caused my heart to burst into its own orgasm.

Joseph's ghost never appeared at any other time. It was never present when I lazed about my apartment, jerking off to my collection of S&M videos. Nor did I sense him when I lay in a lonely bed roughly handling my cock until I came in my hand and took anti-climatic delight in watching my semen creep down the length of my forearm.

It seemed that Joseph only appeared while I was having sex. It was as if he only made himself obvious when there was a third party. Just like the good old days, when Joseph and I brought other guys to my studio—hand-jobbing with rough grasps and sucking the textures of crushed velvet with excited mouths; blending the smooth and painful world of leather into the wee hours of the morning.

Leather—that was the passion we shared together. Both Joseph and I had developed a taste for salty rawhide and an urge for the snapping of tassels on flesh. Mmm, the smooth, black and shiny side that would graze over our defined curves. Oh, the ecstatic wonders of lustful nights.

In life, Joseph was my lover of nine months. He was my best friend, my over-anxious companion, and my traveling partner when we cased Padlock and Club Zero in the overgenerous district of gay Phoenix.

We searched for mirror images of ourselves. Forget the feminine queens; forget the passive pretty boys. We were in search of hardcore, downright rugged men—muscles and powerful thrusts, not low-fat corporate diets. And those men, those bulky and macho men, we could have in our own primal and animalistic grips. We could rip a new rift in the realms of ecstasy with those men. We would make them pay for our days' stresses with every release, make them intimate to every anger we felt with each buck of the hips, and make them cum inside us and all over our strapping bodies.

Joseph himself was quite a catch. Meeting him was probably the best and worst move I could've made. Like pain and pleasure, you can't have one without the other. So it was that I prepared for my longing passions to be fulfilled and then, prematurely, stripped from me.

When I first met him, I lusted for him and wanted him to feel my embrace of power. How I could tightly hug that smooth, hairless body of defined muscle. He was six-foot even (the perfect height) and his sandalwood flesh was accented by chestnut hair. Though short at the back of his scalp, he had light-brown wisps that fully framed his square, unshaven face. His biceps stretched the fabric of his cotton shirts and his jeans were filled with a bulge of considerable size.

If there were one good thing I could say about Joseph in his time with me, it would be: "Could that man fuck!" He was brazen but made it all feel so fantastic at the same time. He used to throw me down onto my bed, take total dominating control, and literally tear the clothes from my body. He'd flip me over on my stomach and jab his cock far into my anus. Preparing me with his same fetish for leather, he would restrain my wrists and ankles to the four posts of my bed with buckled, leather cuffs. Spread-eagle was I, and he would use his domineering force to push down my shoulders, my back, and my ass onto the bed my body would eagerly bounce up from. Heart racing, hardness in my own cock, he'd slide his hands in the crack of my ass and part either side far from each other, his tongue probing the cleft that begged for forgiveness and his face ferociously burrowing in between my tense cheeks. Then, without warning, he would thrust and plummet deep into me, his deliciously solid organ discovering my constricting insides and feeling the hidden country of lust within me. Probing deeper. Oh, hurt me with pain flaring through my entire being. Buckle up; stop! No, go further, for it hurt like acid in my bowels, but it felt so good. Then, harden even more so I can feel the throbbing against my sensitive walls. Release. His heated breath upon the nape of my neck. Stream your life-blood within me. Let me feel it tickle my innards and may it be at least two minutes before it demands to be expelled from my system.

Ah yes, that was the Joseph I knew. Not the ghostly voyeur that had observed my intimate encounters over the past three months. That was the Joseph I remembered—the one who was never too tired for sex and always implemented our fucking to the violent world of a heavy metal song.

At the end of our nine months is when it went so horribly wrong. It seemed that Joseph developed an exclusive love for me. He no longer wanted the company of other men in our bed; no more clubbing for sex objects that we would fuck then forget. And, quite simply, that was it.

There was no other alternative for me, not a shred of respect as to what I wanted. What I didn't want was to settle down like a married couple, as it appeared Joseph wanted. Hell, I'll never settle down. I'm twenty-seven, have a great body, and want the experience of different people, new muscle, and undiscovered cocks.

When Joseph declared his lifelong dedication to me, we were both drunk and at the top of a flight of cement stairs that led to my studio. I was outraged; man was I so full of anger. How could he ask this of me? We exchanged rigid words for the first and last time. Then, perhaps out of instant hatred, I pushed him with both of my hands.

I forcefully landed the palms of my hands against his firm chest and Joseph never had a chance to regain his balance, let alone an opportunity to twist his head and brace himself for the fall that was coming. He fell back, and the sound of his neck made a squishing crunch as the base of his skull met with the first cement platform. He tumbled, his body ricocheting from handrail to handrail down the staircase like a thrown rag doll. By the time he reached the bottom of the stairs, his neck had snapped like a twig and was so contorted that it was wrenched past his shoulders. His last view had been witnessed from the backside of his body.

DOA. Yes, Joseph was declared dead on arrival when the Phoenix PD and emergency crew got to the scene. No doubt about it, Joseph's lifeforce had been catapulted from his body just as his mortal soul had been thrown from his physical shell. Nothing left of Joseph save for upturned eyes that dully glistened from half-open lids. The attending paramedic shook his head in part awe and part disbelief as he placed a latex-gloved hand over Joseph's eyes and gently drew them down over his lifeless white orbs.

I recall a scintillating tear. Was it a final cry or a last hope to cling to the realm of the living? Did it hurt as you watched the world go topsy-turvy for a few brief seconds? Was there pain with each crack of your head against the concrete steps, and was your agony as blissful as being flanked with untreated leather? Was there a teetering pleasure?

Baby blue was the cotton sheet tossed over his corpse. *You, my fucking beauty, are dead. You were the best fuck I ever had.*

As the bitter, liquid world of alcohol consumed my mind, my thought processes attempted to develop a guilty conscience. Had I killed Joseph? I convinced the police that it was an accident, but did I believe my own convictions? I drowned the thought out of my head with a few more shots.

Six months after Joseph's death, I had pretty much forgotten the whole ordeal. I pushed it out of my head like a bad, childhood memory. I had many lovers in the interim and I didn't think twice of comparing them to Joseph; for he was nothing more than the best wet dream I ever had.

I began fucking this guy named Ted. Although Ted was exquisite in between the sheets, he managed to scare me off. Not to mention, he rekindled the questionable thoughts I had of Joseph's death. That was Ted's one drawback. Ted with the short and stocky build; Ted, as many curves and definition as a competitive bodybuilder; Ted, with those fast, rabbitlike hips that could pump away until I exploded into my otherworld of pain and pleasure.

Ted was a firm believer in the laws of the supernatural. In fact, he told me about a spirit in his condo that would wake him in the middle of the night and suck him off. Now, I never knew whether to believe him or just think of him as having a very overactive imagination littered with morbid fantasies. But who was I to judge?

One night in bed, as we lay beside each other, sweat profusely beading across our hard bodies, I though of Ted's translucent lover. In retrospect, my mind revisited Joseph. I asked Ted about ghosts; I asked him how a ghost comes to be, why they haunt people, and how to know if one was around. You know, the questions any normal-yet-curious member of society would ask.

He answered me as if he were an authority on the subject, as if he studied detailed accounts in an illustrious school of parapsychology. Ted proceeded to tell me that a ghost was an earthbound spirit and usually that of a person who had died before their time, either at their own hand or at the hands of someone else.

Suicide. Murder. The latter continually echoed in my conscience.

A constricting lump swelled in my throat and I swallowed hard, still tasting some of Ted's load at the back of my tongue.

He continued, stating that a ghost remains on Earth and does not move into the spirit world until it rights any wrongs bestowed upon it in life.

This horrified me! Was I to believe that Joseph was going to end my life? And when? When would this happen and take place? What's more, did I truly kill him or *was* it an accident? It was imperative that I second-guess this repeatedly.

I asked Ted what that meant. Furthermore, when would it be time for the vengeful spirit to make its move?

Ted said that it could take years, even decades, for a ghost to realize they were dead. "They wander," he said, "confused. Only when they finally come to the realization that they are dead does the actual haunting begin." Ted informed me that the haunting may consist of a flickering shadow from the corner of one's eye. It could be mischievous; on the other hand, it could be malevolent. Ultimately, it could easily drive a man to insanity.

"How do you rid a ghost of your surroundings," I casually asked as if interested and not inquiring for my own possible future need.

To that question, Ted simply laughed. It was a condescending laugh, as if I was the fool and he the authority. He made me feel like I didn't know my asshole from the hole in a ground.

"You will know," he stated.

"How?" I queried again.

"The ghost will let you know."

That statement sent chills down my spine. I trembled, yet I had never cringed from such a subject in my life.

As I forced myself into an uneasy sleep, I caught the first glimpse of what I would grow accustom to in the coming months. I spotted a figure—bulky, with a slightly translucent exterior, like saran wrap. He peered at me, maybe directing hatred toward me because, as I've said before, there was never an emotion that shifted his face. He only gazed, maybe even in an insane jealousy of the man named Ted who lay next to me. My heart beat at an unusually high rhythm and I sealed my eyes shut. In those long moments of darkness, I awaited a gelid touch that would jolt me out of my skin and have me running out the door of my own apartment.

Nothing of that sort transpired. Instead, I fell asleep.

Awakening the next morning, I saw Ted out the door and never bothered to call him or take his calls again.

Eventually, I became regularly aware of my ectoplasmic lover's visits. I brought men home with me and practically depended on Joseph to be there. I knew he'd be intently watching, which I must add is so unlike the man I knew. The man I knew searched with me for threesomes throughout the majority of our relationship. He always wanted to be where the action was. In fact, he wanted to be the center of the action.

Then, finally, it happened.

Last night, after an intense bondage episode with a guy I picked up from Club Zero, Joseph not only appeared in his usual form, but he actually approached me. It was the time I had both eagerly and dreadfully awaited. He had watched, had taken his mental notes, and had learned me. It was his move, and this charged my mind into a state of panic.

Joseph sauntered toward me, each footstep slow and cautious. His bare feet made no more of a sound on the cold, hardwood floor than a feather would. My nameless partner soundlessly slept beside me. I gasped for a breath, a sobering breath that would clear my head of the numerous vodka-tonics I'd earlier consumed.

I moderately rose in my bed, sitting erect with my hands shaking upon my damp thighs. I didn't know whether to be intrigued about Joseph's acknowledgment of me or become enshrouded with dread. Closer he came, and horrifically closer. Screamed, I would have screamed and wakened the guy next to me and maybe, just maybe, Joseph would've disappeared. Maybe he would have exploded into a thousand particles of nothingness, into invisible dust—a cremation of his spectral body.

But no, I couldn't scream. Perhaps I was in shock and literally frozen with fear; for I couldn't voluntarily move any of my limbs. I knew that if I did yell, it would only give way to a temporary gratification. Joseph would've appeared the next night or thereafter when I strapped a new hard body to the four posts of my bed.

Joseph's spirit came to a halt beside the bed. I trembled like a scared kitten; I shook uncontrollably as if I a small child seeing the bogeyman emerge from the closet. It was so new to me, and I was a virgin when it came to fear. In that brief moment, when I saw his clear body begin to kneel beside the bed, I thought: *I'm a grown man! I'm built like a rock, yet this thing that is practically invisible scares the hell out of me.*

I candidly sat waiting as Joseph drew closer. His lips were pressed together as if he were about to plant a kiss of haunting passion upon my cheek.

All sounds muted. No longer could I hear my mysterious lover's snores of deep sleep. Nor could I hear the slight buzzing sound the stereo makes when all music has stopped and the featured disc is over. No sounds at all. No car tires treading on the tarmac of Camelback Road below, no eerie creaks of a modern, synthetic apartment. Nothing. It was as if it were Joseph's moment, as if his voice was to be the only thing the world allowed my ears to register—a meaning, his longing for the afterlife. His request.

"I'm done watching," he whispered in my ear. His voice was so calm, yet echoed as if we were in a deep cavern. I briskly looked over to my partner to see if he'd been awakened by the alien voice. He remained in his deep slumber.

"I want part of the action," Joseph continued. "I want what we used to have: the threesomes, the different men, the two of us. I want it," he requested. Although his voice remained calm, at the same time, it dictated such demand.

Was I hearing him correctly? He wanted it all back? How was I to do this for him? It seemed that Joseph craved sex in his ghostly form as much as he did in the real life he once had. He wanted it all back again, that was what he confided in me. Had I taken it from him? Of course I had. I knew it and he knew it as well. He'd had the last few months to plot his request, to think about what he wanted, and to explore his longings within his lonely realm of solitude. He wasn't seeking a path to his final rest; he was searching for the life he'd once lived. Hell, he didn't want to move on to the Afterlife; he didn't want to leave at all!

"How?" I began to ask, looking at his smooth, unmarred face.

Joseph directed my attention toward the man who lay naked beside me. "His name is Lewis. Have him take you."

"I was a bit confused and aghast. " What? What do you—"

Joseph interjected. "Have him take you, Brent!" This he commanded. His eyes gave off an intimidating darkness. He peered at me, through the flesh and into my thoughts and cells that made my being. The dark hairs on my forearms rose in attention. He would have this one way or another, and he gave me no choice. Joseph made sure to relay that with his gaze of insanity, with his eerie, sardonic smile.

Slight hesitation, then I turned toward the man named Lewis. A virgin shake of the limbs as I prodded my tongue into the ear of my partner fast asleep. "Lewis," I called, trying to wake him. "Fuck me, Lewis."

Lewis took in a great gasp of air as he came to from his world of dreams. He directed his mouth toward mine and plunged his pasty tongue past my lips.

Our tongues danced around in each other's mouths; saliva trickled over Lewis' plump lips. "Take me, Lewis," I pleaded, sounding more as a woman sounds when her sex is throbbing for a man's bulging cock.

No words.

Lewis mounted me and forced my hands down upon the upper corners of the mattress. He casually leaned to the left side of the bed to gather the leather restraints and tassel. In that moment, while the plethora of sex toys and anticipation of which of them he would choose distracted Lewis, I glimpsed over his shoulder to find Joseph.

Joseph was retracting from the tempestuous scene. He was taking small, backward steps into an embracing darkness. The outlining shimmer of his spectral form gradually faded into the blackness of the room. Where was he going?

Lewis viciously attacked my right hand with anxious, black leather and forcefully tied my wrist to the phallic post of the oak headboard. There was an instant heat and a tiny burn from the leather hugging my wrist, like that of a pencil eraser being rubbed back and forth on a hairless forearm. Quick pain, yes! He teased me as he made a wet, sloppy path with his tongue from my shoulder to my stiff nipple. Bite—a sharp pinch that caused me to writhe beneath my dominator and involuntarily fend him off with my free hand. Lewis didn't allow it. He briskly grabbed my other hand and made a duplicate gesture of the first binding. Tie it tightly, yes! Then the legs—he spread my legs and bound each ankle to its respective bedpost, but not before pressing his tongue to the base of my swollen cock.

Lewis applied immense pressure with his tongue as he slid it up my long, pulsing shaft, stopping at the perfectly circumcised head and circling it with wet traces. Then he swallowed it in deep gulps. Once. Twice. Swallowing it whole the third time, my balls tingled. Five, six, seven times—entirely and with precision. Stop! Make it last, Lewis; make it feel even better!

Like a mind reader, he pulled his mouth from my cock and it gently grazed every fiber of his lips.

Lewis drew back his arm through the faint darkness and leather tassels landed upon my face. They brushed past my eyes and tickled my nose. The smell was salty and new for only just this time. How those deep brown tassels would taste. How masculine—a taste of powerful cum. Without warning, he withdrew the leather from my face. The smooth and rough texture smacked against my chest. I could take it; it turned me on even more. Again, a snap to my chest and I felt lust! I felt solid; I felt anger. I wanted to rape this man teasing me, as my cock grew wildly hardened with magnificent pulses. Next was the stomach. Lewis slapped the leather hard, and I tightened my abdominal muscles. It tickled and, at the same time, burned. Ah, the wonders! Again and again, a wondrous feeling of rawhide against vulnerable flesh.

Lewis continued for the next half hour—snaps of leather upon my chest and stomach, fervent biting at my nipples, dark hairs crunching between clenched teeth as he took mouthfuls of my muscle between his lips. My cock was so hard that it hurt, and the tiniest bit of pre-cum emerged from the tip as Lewis slid up and down my shaft with his prostate. I could feel the warmness of my cum; my cock grazed the slimy pocket of fluid that had spilt near the base of Lewis' tight balls. Sweat beaded on my biceps and trickled into my armpits. I was wet and refreshingly cool.

As I drifted into my euphoric state, Lewis must have grabbed the tube of lubricant; for I rushed back into real consciousness from the gelid touch of his finger playfully toying with my hole. He cautiously slid one finger in and I moaned with slight agony. Partially in, he maneuvered the prodding digit and, with the same ease, pulled it out. In once more, deep and gently. Next, his middle finger. Lewis combined his index and middle fingers and dexterously moved them into my anus. The burn, oh! I wanted to scream at him to take his free hand and stroke my cock. Stroke it hard and make the tingling pleasures subside the minor flaring within my body. I attempted using my own hand but, as much as I pulled it from the mast to which it was bound, the binding seemed to grip tighter rather than leave room for my wrist to slip out.

I began bucking beneath my seducer. I moved in a heated motion, synchronizing my buttocks with his plunging fingers. It hurt, yet it felt wondrous.

Suddenly the thought emerged: *where was Joseph?* No sooner than I mentally asked, did Joseph's ghost emerge from the shadows.

The outline of Joseph's broad shoulders materialized. There came the oval-shaped head, that trim thirty-one inch waist and, finally, the lower half was present. Although the ghost stood within a few feet from the base of the bed, barely taller than Lewis who rocked back and forth upon my cock, I could not make out Joseph's face. There was only a faint outline, bluish gray in color, a barely visible tracer against the friendly darkness of the bedroom.

I remained in a frenzied lust and seduced by fear as well. I knew not what expression carved Joseph's face. The two emotions jolted my heart into an intense drugged rhythm. My entire body tingled with the overflow of adrenal juices, and trembled in mystery.

Surely, the look on my haunt's face couldn't have been what I was used to seeing. After all, this was Joseph's move in this strategic game of lust. This was his request as I had carried out for him, and now was the true moment of his enigmatic plan.

Was his expression that of hatred, for hatred of what I had done to him? Was there an evil face, contorted by death, awaiting me? The mystery was killing me, though I remained hard for Lewis. My god, what was Joseph going to do?

Lewis interrupted my mind adrift in awe. "I'm gonna fuck you so hard, Brent. You want that?"

"Oh, yeah," I automatically responded in programmed feedback. My attention shifted back to Lewis.

Lewis removed his fingers from my anus. He took the thumb and index finger of both hands and tightly pinched my nipples, half twisting them. At the same time, he pummeled his penis into the orifice that his two fingers had just finished preparing.

Lewis' dick was rather small and thin, prickly in the literal sense, yet it still produced a faint burn within my ass. He continued twisting my swollen nipples and moved his cock in and out of me. For some reason, both pains began to dull my libido. Perhaps the combination of the two began to annoy me. It seemed that Lewis just couldn't do it right. I mean, the guy gave a great blowjob, but he was a lousy fuck.

Abruptly, Lewis stopped his pelvic thrusts. My eyes fluttered open from my semi-pleasured state and I peered up at Lewis' face. I observed droplets of sweat rolling down a face frozen with confusion. Lewis looked as if one of our parents had broken into the apartment and caught us in the act. It was as if he sensed something, or somebody, behind him. Sense, yes. At that point, I knew he must have noticed Joseph's presence. I watched as he made a furtive turn of his head, not sure if he wanted to see what stood behind him.

Lewis' cock was still inside me. My body attempted to expel it from my insides. I studied in complete suspense as my heart began to race faster.

Before Lewis had a chance to turn his head, I caught a fleeting glimpse of Joseph's face—almond flesh ignited in the dark, eyes burning with determination, lips pursed.

I gawked in terror at the scene becoming. It happened so quickly, like the premature cumming of a cock withdrawn from abstinence. I believe Lewis was about to yelp; however, the scream that began to emit from his throat was stifled, instantly cut-off.

The hellbent face of Joseph glowered down at Lewis. Joseph placed both of his transparent hands upon Lewis' heaving shoulders. Lewis could only close his eyes in shock and remain silent. I gazed as specks of brilliant light emerged from Joseph's iridescent body. Electric blues, emerald greens, golds, ruby reds, and silvers—all these colors spat from Joseph's ghost and poured down upon Lewis' flesh. It was an electrical parade of wonder, a Fourth of July grand finale, a miracle in the making.

I could no longer see the ghost.

The glittering specks of color fell gently over Lewis like a light snow. A dusting of Joseph all over my awestruck lover, and those tiny particles of his ghost burrowed their way into Lewis' skin. Through every pore, the phenomenon seeped into him until Lewis was Lewis no more.

A pain shot through my anal cavity; it felt as if the cock within me grew in length and girth. Bulging and growing harder. Filling me. Him. It was Joseph's cock filling me, I realized. I studied Lewis' frozen expression. He was stock-still as a statue and just as stiff. He opened his eyes and dread enshrouded my every fiber.

I writhed beneath my lover and tried to expel his massive cock; for those eyes were a familiar blue. Crystalline eyes. Joseph's eyes.

"No," I screamed. And it no longer mattered that I would consider myself meager from my cries; it no longer made a difference that I may feel inferior to the rest of the world (for the first time). After all, my masculinity was being devoured, and I was a victim. Yes, for once the victim, and I couldn't react because I had never known what it was like or how it felt to be a victim to anything.

Fleeting glimpses of everything I'd ever done or hoped to do flashed through my mind. Then, the uncanny thought of a ghost possessing the body of a living person struck me with wonder.

"Relax, Brent," Joseph's voice soothingly stated. "I want to fuck you."

Joseph manipulated Lewis' body. It was still Lewis' body, with the exception of the enormous cock that drilled deep and those enrapturing, blue eyes.

He thrust himself into me, guiding his cock in and out of me with a comforting, yet painful force. Once again, more than anything, I wanted to free my own hands and stroke my dick. I wanted to cum so badly; God, I thought I could explode from the most gracious touch!

In and out, back and forth, and with perfect rhythm. The hand of Lewis grasped my throbbing shaft and handled it with extreme roughness. Then he retracted, spit into his hand, and rubbed his saliva up and down my cock. My entire body was about to convulse and rupture into orgasm!

Quicker he pumped his hips into me, all the while stroking me harder. His palm clasped the head of my cock and he skillfully slid in down to the base. I felt an elation of none ever experienced as the sensation of semen bubbling and ticking at the base of my engorged organ became present. Oh yes; like a massive volcano ready to erupt, slower it crept toward the top, ready to spill over at any time.

Harder. I wanted Joseph to fuck me harder. I pulled at the restraints and wanted to tear into Lewis' ass and pull him further into me. I wanted everything of him inside of me. It felt wonderful! This was fantastic; this was bliss. Thrusting and thrusting, I began to observe the sweat that trickled from his forehead. That was my Joseph! Yes, that was the way he did it, and I would give every night to have him possess any body he wanted to so long as I could retain this excitement.

Suddenly, the supernaturally animated body stopped. It became a dead weight against my inner thighs. I was just about to release when Lewis' possessed body came to an abrupt halt. What the hell was he doing, teasing me? Did Joseph want to punish me that badly?

My heavy breathing slowed, as did the breath that came from Lewis. *Joseph's breath.*

A wicked silence pervaded the room. I frightfully jerked when Joseph's voice spoke. "You know, I could kill you right now, Brent."

No, please. God, please no! I didn't know if I could take any more; I felt my heart was going to explode with unquenchable fear.

"Yes, Brent, just as quickly as you did me. One second was all it took for you to force your hands onto my chest."

I was flabbergasted and searched for words. My cock still pulsed with an urge to cum. "No," I answered, "I didn't mean to—"

"But you did," Joseph interrupted my apology. He glowered at my helpless body as if in heavy contemplation. What was he planning to do? "But as I told you before," he continued, "I want a part of the action, and that's exactly what I'm going to get."

He began moving his cock out of me; my prostate became soar and lusting at the same time. Suddenly, he powerfully drove it back into me. He resumed stroking my cock; his grip became tighter with each caress. He pushed it in; oh yeah, more! He placed his cool hands upon my belly and it felt refreshing.

Faster he prodded into me. I observed the confused emotion of hatred and lust blended, as it stemmed from the man that Joseph had taken control.

He rubbed my cock in brisk, long strokes. I reached the threshold of orgasmic explosion. A moan of pleasure poured over his lips the way I remembered Joseph sexually crying.

I ejaculated like never before. A thick stream of semen exploded from my cock, arced through the heated air, and splattered onto my chest, neck, and stomach. I convulsed from euphoric rushes that sped throughout my body. I wanted to melt; I could feel the warm cum trickle down into the deep groove of my chest.

Another wave of ecstasy crashed into me as Joseph manipulated Lewis' hips into one final, deep thrust that sparked his release into me. I could feel the involuntary contracting of his throbbing penis. Pulsing and squirting, his cum shot into me and filled me with a comfort I once knew.

For the life of me, I cannot describe the feeling that came over me. It was as if a piece of Joseph resided within me, his ectoplasmic semen traveling and tickling my insides.

I fell asleep with Lewis' body draped over mine as I slipped out of the conscious mind with an uncanny force writhing inside me. I entered a night of dreams with my last thought being that of confining restraints.

When I woke this morning, Lewis had already left. I can't say I don't blame him. How thankful I am that he removed the leather straps that bound me.

So here I am…back to a life thrown off its course for a while. I sit at the bar of Club Zero. I can't help but notice the exquisite man leaning back against the opposing wall. He casually stands there—deep espresso, fauxhawk-shaped hair, an overly tight T-shirt that exposes every ripple of his muscular chest, and jeans that grip around his cock to prove his manhood—observing the throng of dancers

I remember Joseph saying he "wanted part of the action." Just like the good old days. I believe we are as one now, and he can relive all the threesomes and robust bodies that we used to share. We seek out men together; we feel stinging snaps of leather together; we cum together.

Together, as one.

As for his request to be exclusively with me—the wish that prompted his death—I suppose he got that one too.

"He's a good one," Joseph says.

I answer him back in my mind because that's how I hear him. And although he is inside of me and at ease, I dread the day a struggle emerges for us to part. "Yeah, let's take him home," I say.

A Cub's Tail

cub[1] (*noun*) – A term used in gay circles to describe a young, hairy gay man. Essentially, a young bear.

Father had always been my only love.

As a child, I felt the world would uncontrollably spin off its axis, and I would be cast into outer space, had it not been for Father's constant grasp. His large forearms would easily encircle my narrow shoulders as we walked to the corner store for Father's cigarettes. In my impressionable, pre-adolescent mind, I knew I would become a smoker when I grew older. After all, I was fascinated by the way the cigarette smoke from Father's mouth whirled out, as if a hypnotic fog coming into bay. I adored the image of the blue-gray swirls against Father's olive skin framed by a full black beard. To me, I saw art. I saw a man I loved.

When I was a teenager, Father used to always play-wrestle with me. I absolutely loved it—the way his burly structure gave no struggle as he threw me to my back within the overgrown grass in our yard, and how the combination of his facial whiskers and arm hair scraped against my silky face as they battled to pin one of my shoulder's to the ground. My scrawny stature could never compete with the stalwart force of Father's body. And when I thought I had the opportunity to get the win on him (using the maneuver of tickling his bushy armpits), I found myself anxious to give in to Father's domineering force. This was mostly common when we wrestled shirtless. Even in the moment of victory, I overthrew the playful match to allow Father's shaggy torso to meet my pubescent skin. Oh how I treasured the feel of Father's curly hairs against my sleek flesh!

My love for Father never died, even when he did.

***

As I gaze across the sea of prettyboys, their hips gyrating to the latest techno-babble dance music, I find deliverance. The wildly spinning lights briefly capture his features as they continuously accentuate the half-naked patrons who party into an ecstasy-induced trance.

"Father," I mutter.

[1]Urban Dictionary

"What?" an inebriated man slurs.

I glance to my left as I place my empty glass upon the bar. The chubby face of a drunken Hispanic meets me. I am disgusted by the spit that hangs from his plump lower lip, like that of an animal with an appetite for its prey. How I remember that look of hunger for sex. And it never mattered how the other person appeared. Forget the formalities; forget the niceties. Meaningless fucking. That's all it ever is. *Was.*

As if, I mentally say. I could say it aloud and hurt the ugly beast's feelings. After all, the past eight years without Father have been lonely. The years have been filled with nothing but drunken and forced sexual encounters with beasts. The beasts know their prey well. They know that loneliness leads to self-pity and self-pity leads to low self-esteem. Hell, I've been fucked by nothing but hideous men. Just stay behind me; don't let me see your face. Place your hairy chest against the smooth contours of my back. Fill me up with your wild and hungry cock while I think of him. I always think of Father so that I can feel that much closer to him.

***

It was rather sudden, Father's death. He was only forty-three years old, and I was but seventeen. He collapsed one evening, right after a fight with Mother.

Mother. What a bitch!

Mother had come down on Father all the time in those final two years. Those were the years when Mother discovered the Bible. She began saying grace before every meal (though Father and I started eating regardless) and she prayed on her knees, at the foot of her and Father's bed, every night before she went to sleep. Although Mother claimed to have found Christ again, I think she was bored with her life. After all, I had always felt a sense of jealousy when she watched Father and I play. It showed in her cruel, espresso-colored (almost black) eyes that could easily pierce the coldest of bitches. I think she had always wanted a daughter.

Nonetheless, it didn't warrant her outbursts at Father. How fucking Christian was that? "Hey," she would always call after him. She never called him by his name, James; nor did she ever get his attention by saying "Husband", the way she used to playfully joke in the years before I entered puberty. No. It was always, "Hey, your cigarette smoke's bothering me," (an overdramatic, fake cough would always follow) or "Hey, why the hell are you drinking a beer on a Tuesday night." Father drank beer, but not to the point of alcoholism. It was a beer here and there. Just enough to keep buzzed, enough to stay even when Mother's word weaponry came blazing.

Although Father never yelled at Mother (he was rather passive in confrontations with her), there were times when I wanted to be his voice. I wanted to scream out to my Mother, "Hey, why don't you stop yelling at Father, you bitch!" or "Hey, why don't you get a life and live a little, you cunt!" But no; I simply stood, silently listening from behind my bedroom door as she verbally attacked Father. All the while, I felt sorrow for Father; I imagined his eyes ignited with a sadness that only Mother could bring on.

Father was often gone, presumably at a local bar. This, I'm sure, so that Mother wouldn't bitch and moan about his smoking or drinking. Aside from his work at the factory and his time with me (while Mother worked part-time as a grocery store clerk), this was his only peace.

That fateful night of his death, he'd just returned from a bar and Mother scolded him. She accused him of cheating on her. Once again, these were Mother's own insecurities. She told him he was going to Hell for infidelity. Father yelled! I couldn't believe it. For once, Father had yelled at her. I mentally applauded from the confines of my bedroom as I heard Father's raised voice for the first and only time.

"Just leave me the fuck alone, Candice!"

Mother gasped. "What-did-you-say? What-did-you-say-to-*me*?" Mother accentuated each word clearly, pausing before the next.

"Just get away from me," Father hollered.

That's when I heard it. THUD! It echoed through the house and brought the raised voices to an abrupt silence. I could hear my own breathing.

"Hey," Mother called. "Hey, get up!" Then, there was a brief silence before I heard Mother's voice again. "Yes, I need an ambulance right away. My husband just fell unconscious."

Slowly, I opened my bedroom door. I immediately saw Father. He laid face first upon the hallway floorboards. His eyelids were fluttering closed, sealing off the cinnamon hue of his irises. His chest did not heave. His body made not a movement. Instantly, I went into shock. My body trembled uncontrollably. My mouth remained agape. All the while, somewhere in the deep recesses of my frightened and fragile mind, I couldn't believe that this seemingly unbreakable man lay before me. It wasn't possible!

Father, please don't be dead. Come back to me.

I thought I saw his parted lips come together to produce a thin smile.

The next day, Mother had attempted to explain Father's passing to me. She said that the doctors claimed Father had suffered from a stroke. There was no sincerity to her uncaring words that etched lines of cruelty around her mouth. In fact, she almost appeared happy.

I didn't believe Mother. I didn't think Father had passed away at all. After all, Mother didn't take me to the funeral. She said that it would be "too difficult" for me. No, Father wasn't dead. Perhaps he was dead to Mother. God, how I hated her!

***

"You are sooooo fiiiiine!" the Hispanic man says in an attempt to grab hold of my attention.

I don't even bother to acknowledge the lush. For across the throng of shirtless bodies, *he* captivates me. He stands still as a statue, above the pit of the dance floor and simply gazing. It's as if he is indecisive in his next movement, as if he's ready to exit the club.

Don't leave!

I begin to walk away from the bar and manage to spill half of my martini as I repeatedly graze shoulders with others who are standing in various unformed lines to order their drinks. I keep him in sight as he slightly turns to the left and reveals his profile. The bright, revolving strobes ignite his face for brief moments. I observe his full beard, his dull jaw line, and Romanesque nose.

I know it's you! Please don't leave!

Suddenly, I'm a child again. It's as if the entire club slows to a crawl. The upbeat, synthesized treble of the music falls to a tiresome, bass-induced thud. The movement of the swarming bodies that dance all about decelerates into endless, undulating waves. I'm a child and I'm running after the ice cream truck that's about to exit the neighborhood. I'm looking down at my feet as I race to reach the school bus before the folding entrance shuts me out. I can't trip. I'm almost there! I'm a child and I'm scrambling towards Father as he enters the house from a long day at work.

I casually ease my stride as I reach *him.*

Sensing my presence, he turns toward me and we are facing each other. The multi-colored lights shine upon our faces and giddiness stirs my stomach. We are saints, he and I—the luminescence haloing our heads. I catch a lighted glance of his eyes as the atmosphere around me comes up to speed. His irises are the color of cinnamon.

"Hi," I hasten.

He continuously looks me up and down as if he a scientist and I his specimen. "Uh, hi," he responds. I watch his thin lips form each word.

I reach out my finger and push it against his husky chest. The muscle is taut beneath the dark fleece of hair upon the surface of his olive flesh.

"You all right? Are you drunk?"

I snap from my obvious reverie of freakishness and laugh. "Yes, I'm fine," I say. "I spilt my drink along the way."

"Ahhh," he smiles. "You were checking me out while I was deciding who to check out. Was that it?"

"I suppose so." An awkward silence quickly eclipses the conversation. "I'm Denny."

"I'm James." He extends his hand.

I can't stop staring at his chest. I'm lost in an ocean of tightly curled hairs, of dark yet calming waters. I want to reach out and run my fingers through every wiry strand. I want to lap at them with my tongue. *James*, he said.

"Father," I whisper.

"Excuse me?"

"Nothing." I change the subject. "Wanna dance?"

"How 'bout we go back to my place?"

My limbs beam with a thousand tingly sensations. Oh, how I must go with him, must be with him. *Father, it's Denny. Father, I've waited so long.*

"Sure," I immediately agree.

James grabs my hand and begins leading me out of the club. I want to feel him against me, his chest against mine.

In the car, on the way back to James' place, I do all I can to refrain from staring at him. I observe his gaze at the street before us, that same intensity with which Father used to have when meticulously putting together his muscle car model collection. I study James' bulky forearms and the mass of dark hairs that practically cover them black. I revel in the way the overhead streetlights illuminate James' almond flesh, giving his forehead a sickly pale tint.

Twice, James notices my watchful eyes. Twice, he asks, "You all right?"

My response is, "Yes."

The third time, I quickly turn my head as he is, once again, distracted by my observing him. I stare out the window, and a burst of adrenaline causes my heart to gallop. Everything outside of the vehicle slows to a crawl as I examine the convenient store that we pass. Although the color of the building has gone from white to tan over the years, that same recognizable signage has not changed. I make out the words: Francisco's Corner Market. That is the store Father and I used to walk to for his cigarettes! I used to live in that neighborhood!

I peer back as we pass the store, and now I know that this is really happening. *Father! I'm coming, Father.*

This time, when I glance over at James, his eyes remain on the road. Yet, a familiar smirk forms upon his lips.

James' apartment is meticulous and smells like *Febreze*. The aroma of freshly clean linen permeates the atmosphere. The cherry wood coffee table and entertainment center brilliantly shine, absent of any dust. The cleanliness reminds me of the same way Father would keep the family room.

It is no coincidence that I am here. Surely, Father has sought me out. He has heard my midnight whispers as I fall to an uneasy sleep, has been in my dreams when the imagery of he and I frolicking plays like a soothing lullaby. He has been in touch with my hopeful emotions that throw me into a state of depression, weakening my mind and body. After, eight years, he has come back as James. Perhaps, he has returned before now and has been relentlessly seeking me.

It matters not the circumstances. What does matter is that I am here now, in this apartment that smells of the old family room in which Father I would sit and watch scary movies. What matters is that I now stand in the center of James' apartment and stare directly into his eyes. I study the cinnamon swirls that peer back at me, capturing me in an ecstasy that ignites my stomach with butterflies.

There is no conversation. James leans in and plants his dry lips upon mine. He brushes his cheek against mine; the hair upon his jaw tickles the side of my face as if they squirm with a life of their own. James pulls back and I stare at his full beard. The curls transfix me; I'm hypnotized by the subtle movement the black hairs appear to make as they overlap one another. So this is our reunion; this is our fated assembly.

"I know who you are," I break the silence.

"Of course you do," he says. "I told you my name, remember?"

"No, I know who you *really* are."

"Do you, now?" James cocks his head to the right, analyzing my discovery of his identity.

"Yes, Father."

One of James' eyebrows shifts into an arc. "Father, huh?"

"It's all right;" I assure, "I've been waiting for you a long time, Father. You have no clue how many nights I prayed for your return. The tears and the pain, it was all worth it. You're here now, and I will remain by your side forever."

"You want to be with me forever?" James pulls up his shirt over his head, revealing a defined chest and flat stomach covered with thick, inky hairs. He pushes down his jeans and underwear, and a mass of overgrown hairs greets me.

I walk toward him. "Yes, forever." I bury my lips into his chest, licking the hairs that blanket his flesh.

James places his hands on either of my shoulders and gently pushes me back. "If you want to be with me forever, then fuck me."

For a moment, I cringe from the seriousness of his squinting eyes. Then, I quickly disrobe so that I am standing naked before him.

James grabs both of my hands and pulls me toward him. I watch the black hairs on his chest wiggle and come to life. Each hair individually grows erect and sways back and forth in unison, as if a subtle breeze is blowing the sea of hair. Apparently, somebody had slipped something into my drink at the bar. The last time this happened, I got sick to my stomach and puked on the back of the guy I was fucking. Yet, my stomach is not upset. Instead, the tickling sensations of excitement extend from the inside of my belly out to the rest of my limbs like an amazing adrenalin rush. It's as if I'm riding a rollercoaster that is slowly creeping up to a crest before revealing the fast-paced, downward drop.

I let go of James' hands and move around his side, to his back. The hairs upon his shoulders and back begin dancing, as if they magnetized to my flesh. My hands cup the half-orbs of his ass, and I take in a quavering breath from the feeling of the soft tufts of hair that cover the area. Instantly, I feel myself grow erect. I grab around either side of James and push my cock into his ass.

Warmth. I encounter a soothing heat that fills my body with the comfort only a child can understand, one that alleviates his mind in knowing that his parent loves him. *To be with you, Father. Yes!* I thrust into

James again, and the young man begins to hum unintelligible words. Of the words I can make out, I hear 'Adeo' and 'Vita.'

Our movement becomes like that of a synchronized wave—my thrusting and his hips greeting my pelvis create a harmonized flow as if we are dancefloor lusts at a club moving to the driving force of techno beats. My excitement brims, and I am close to release. But, I don't want to lose this feeling, want to feel it forever.

As I continue to buck my hips into James', my backside begins tickling and itching. I feel myself pulled deeper into James' ass, and my thrusts cease as I look down. My heart bursts into galloping beats as I observe the wiry hairs of James' buttocks wrapping around my waist and ass. Analyzing the phenomenon further, I gasp as I see more of the tendril-like hairs emit from inside of James' and grow in length to encircle my backside. "What's happening?" I yell to James.

His reply consists of nothing more than the words that continue pouring from his mouth, words that sound like some incomprehensible Latin chant.

Surely, this has to be the side effects of a drug slipped to me earlier!

I try to pull from James, but the moving mass of wrapping hairs pushes my hips further into James' buttocks. My erection is forced into his hole. I grab onto his shoulders, and the hairs there grow like weeds that wrap around my wrists and cuff me. All the hairs upon his back begin shooting from his follicles, tickling my chest, and inching down to my waist. It is as if a black web embraces me, the stringy hairs stretching from his back and to my hips as if strings attached to a marionette. I am trapped; a horde of writhing hairs encompasses me.

A hollow crack from my lower vertebrate is loud against James' humming chant. A stabbing agony infiltrates both my upper and lower body. I scream as I feel my back and legs arch back toward one other. "It hurts, Father! It hurts!" However, all I hear are the sounds of James' enigmatic chants.

The hairy cuffs emitting from James' shoulders release my wrists. For a moment, I feel freedom. Before I can reach my hands for James' head, to get his attention, my wrists are briskly pulled back behind my head by the impossible strength of James' wiry hairs. More cracks infiltrate the atmosphere. More chants accentuate the uncanny beats of my breaking back. *No, Father!*

My cock is limp. My hips no longer buck. Before my arms and legs go numb, I think my fingers touch my toes. The upper and lower halves of my body are horizontal with each other as some unexplained force tugs at my crotch.

James is no longer chanting. A slurping replaces his hums.

An abundance of comforting heat greets my waist, crotch, stomach and lower back. It crawls and massages the body. I realize that James' anal orifice is pulling in my entire body, but I almost feel at rest. I am calm as my upper body and calves slide into a wet hole of wonder. A smooth texture that feels like hot pudding allows me to glide into him effortlessly. The putrid smells of shit accost my nostrils before the dim lights of the apartment eclipse the world I know. The creamy texture consumes my face and feet as the world goes black.

Blackness. It is like the emptiness within my heart. I feel you now, Father. I feel you cradling me with heavy, wet hair comforting me. It is as if I am a child in your womb. Sometimes I hear you sing, Father. Although I don't recognize the hollow sounds of your rhythmic humming, I know that you are singing to me. I knew you would come back, Father. Now, we hold each other in the darkness. Forever.

Much of Madness, More of Sin

The bulky doors of St. Sebastian's Cathedral swung inward as Jase and Kyle floated in. The heroin eagerly surged through their veins and, although their consciences solidified the reality that they were grounded by each step they had taken upon the marble floor of the church, their movement was ethereal and without boundaries. The giddiness that filled their stomachs ignited a silent laughter between the young men before Kyle gazed upward at the high-vaulted ceiling and imagined he could fly to it. *Yes, to be up there dangling from those beams! To touch the ceiling, to touch the moon!* Kyle envisioned himself during a Sunday mass, watching the many churchgoers sitting in the pews beneath him as he hovered high above them like a saint, just like a god being worshiped.

Jase was wrestling with paranoia, and it caused his heart to speed more rapidly than it already was. He scanned the inside of St. Sebastian's for any sign of another person. He had been to the cathedral once before, during the midnight hour. Yet, he didn't want to chance being caught, especially given the condition in which he and Kyle were. Still, this was the best time to visit the church and show Kyle the discovery he'd recently made that fueled his obsession.

The dozens of varnished pews on either side of Jase were vacant of any worshipers. To the left of the altar, countless tiny flames danced upon the wicks of votive candles. Jase never understood why churches allowed burning candles to go unattended, but they appeared contained in a fashion that would prevent any such fire hazard. Jase knew of the Catholic tradition and recognized that each flame that flickered, every candle that slowly burned, had been lit for a loved one. However, Jase wasn't Catholic. He didn't believe in Heaven or Hell or even Purgatory for that matter. But he did believe in Jesus Christ. Oh, how he believed in Jesus!

Jase's attention fell back to Kyle whose arm was stretched toward the ceiling. "Kyle," he sternly whispered.

Kyle snapped from his fantastic reverie. "What?" His sharp, squinted eyes conveyed agitation by Jase's disturbance of his daydream.

"Let's shut the doors before somebody comes."

Kyle rolled his eyes as he closed one of the swinging doors and Jase the other. He still didn't know why he'd bothered to follow Jase here in the first place. Then again, he shared many things with Jase—from beds to needles to the men they'd take home together. They weren't boyfriends, but close friends. The relationship they maintained was both that of best friends who trusted one another in sharing every idiosyncrasy of their lives and as fuck buddies when either of them was horny and unable to lure a guy off the dance floor at Club Phenom. Jase referred to this, as it was commonly known among the culture, as "friends with benefits."

Kyle soon recognized that sharing in such "benefits" meant he would be repeatedly subjected to Jase's latest sexual obsession for lanky men. At first, when Jase had announced his fetish, Kyle thought that by the term "lanky", Jase meant thin men with boyish features. Kyle had dropped out of high school his sophomore year and often felt stupid when it came to the many words and terms that were common to the everyday graduate. However, he soon understood what his friend meant while Jase thumbed through one of his many photobooks a few months previous. The pictures contained within were those of tall, naked, and almost skeletal young men. The photography depicted such characteristics as hollowed eyes, high cheekbones, and concaved stomachs that gruesomely exposed ribs.

Kyle had a difficult time comprehending Jase's fixation of such imagery. Jase had always told him how he'd adored Kyle's toned body that mimicked that of an Abercrombie and Fitch model. When Jase fucked him, he'd take pleasure of lapping at the deep crevice between Kyle's well-developed pectorals and running his hands over Kyle's bulging abdominal muscles. Kyle shared in that same bliss as he treated Jase's body in analogous fashion. Though Jase's stomach revealed a slight paunch, Kyle found him incredible to look at. Kyle would run his fingers through Jase's semi-lengthy, blond spikes and stare into his hatchet sharp face emphasized by captivating, hazel eyes. Oh, the wonder and mystery that lay within those luminous eyes!

So why the gangly fascination? Why the recent obsession with skeletons bearing taut flesh? Of the men Kyle and Jase shared—and there were many—none bore such traits. Nevertheless, Jase's fetish led them to St. Sebastian's Cathedral. That's why Kyle suggested they shoot up before arriving there. He found the idea rather boring, to sexually praise an image such as Jesus Christ. What was Jase going to do, masturbate to the man on the cross? Jase insisted that Jesus was the sexiest man in the world, and he begged Kyle to admire the holy icon with him. Kyle would rather be at the club, finding a young, vivacious man, like himself, to take home and fuck all through the night. There was no telling what was to transpire in this place. However, he couldn't decline Jase's invitation. After all, they shared everything.

***

Two years before he met Jase, Kyle murdered a man. It wasn't intentional; Kyle told him not to use the full chamber in one fix.

"Where are we going?"

"Come on," Kyle yelled back at the young man. "We're going into the alley."

There was no way Kyle could wait to take Travis back to his apartment. He had to have him now. God, he was so cute with those cobalt eyes and fleshy lips. Kyle loved how Travis' mouth locked with his on the dance floor and their tongues darted back in forth, driven by the trance music that pummeled the atmosphere of sex and sweat all around them.

Kyle stopped halfway down the alley and pushed Travis against the stucco wall that composed the structure of Club Phenom. Kyle anxiously forced his mouth over Travis' and grinded his hips into the young man, in sync with the muffled beats of the music.

"Damn, I want you so bad," Kyle eagerly exhaled as he pulled from Travis.

"I want you too," the young man responded. "Wanna go back to your place."

Kyle's laughter echoed throughout the alleyway. "I can't wait that long." He licked his lips. "I'm going to take you on a magical ride, baby. Right here, right now. Junk and all, you're going to fucking love it!"

The youth in Travis' eyes beamed excitement like one unexpected to a surprise birthday gift. "You have some?"

"Oh yeah," Kyle excitedly stated as he reached into his jacket and pulled out a prepared hypodermic along with a rubber cord. The yellow substance within the chamber of the hypodermic glistened beneath the dimness of a nearby streetlight.

Travis pulled his long-sleeved shirt over his head and threw it to the ground. His small nipples grew hard from the cold, January winter.

Kyle licked around one of Travis' nipples then gently bit at it. He took the black rubber cord and began wrapping it around the base of the young man's unnoticeable bicep. Kyle observed the hunger in Travis' bulging eyes and planted a brisk kiss upon the youth's lips.

The young man giggled uncontrollably, as if being tickled. "What's your name again?"

Kyle wasn't fazed by the question and continued wrapping the cord around Travis' thin arm. "I'm your man of illusions. Remember? We're going on a magical ride."

Travis smiled in acknowledgment.

"See that star up there?" Kyle gestured with his eyes toward the cosmos.

"The bright one?"

"Yeah."

"Uh-huh," Travis impatiently nodded his head.

"That's where we're gonna go."

"Really?"

"Yeah, and we're going to fuck all the way there."

Travis sniggered with enthusiasm as he watched Kyle find a vein with the tip of the needle.

"Now, I'm going to give you half first and I'll take the other half," Kyle instructed.

"I bet if I had the whole thing, I could fly farther than that star; I could go to Venus," Travis childishly mocked.

"Uh, no," Kyle firmly stated. "If you shot the entire chamber, you'd probably overdose. You ready?"

Travis winced as Kyle inserted the needle into the crook of Travis' arm. Soon, his heart fluttered in excitement and he leaned forward to kiss Kyle. Their tongues danced within each other's mouth as Kyle slowly pushed the contents of the chamber into Travis' vein. Kyle's eyes measured the emptying chamber as he continued kissing Travis. Damn, this boy was ready to go; he couldn't wait to be inside of him.

Without warning, as Kyle was distracted by making love to the young man before him, Travis' free hand swiftly moved atop of the thumb of Kyle's that administered the heroin. Travis pushed down hard so that the rest of the chamber could be emptied into his veins.

Kyle pulled back and yanked the needle from Travis' arm. Travis roared "Fuck!" from the pain of the hypodermic being violently pulled out. Then Travis anxiously unwrapped the cord that constricted his bicep and put his head against the wall.

"What the fuck did you do that for?" Kyle screamed. But he knew the kid wasn't listening because his eyelids were flickering as the rush came.

"Ohhhhhh," Travis breathed in ecstasy. The giddiness that tickled the boy's stomach traveled to his legs and arms. He wanted to laugh, and that made him want to laugh more. The delightful sensation crawled up into his chest and his eyes rolled back in his head. He felt light, yet his body heavily fell to the ground.

"Travis!" Kyle quietly yelled, trying not to bring any attention to any passerby who entered the club. But it was to know avail, for Travis slumped over as his eyes remained open.

Kyle quickly checked the boy's pulse but couldn't locate the slightest beat. Oh god, he thought, oh my god! Kyle's heart raced into horrific panic as he fled down the alley, refusing to look back at the lifeless corpse of the kid with whom he was going to fly to the stars.

***

Jase and Kyle glided down the center aisle of St. Sebastian's. Jase's eyes remained transfixed on the large crucifix that hovered above the altar. It was the biggest crucifix he'd ever seen; it had to be at least ten feet tall, and the replica of the crucified form of Jesus Christ was that of life-size. Jase had never witnessed a full-scale Jesus Christ model such as the one in St. Sebastian's. He imagined touching the thin arms that stretched out to either side of the cross. *Such tender flesh!* Jase reveled in the thoughts of running his hand over the concaved stomach of Jesus and reaching down into his dainty loincloth. Oh, how he would love to suck on his cock and be inside of the savior, breaking Christ's lanky body with each hard thrust! Jase felt the bulge in his jeans grow firmer with each step he took toward the altar.

Kyle followed Jase down the aisle, mesmerized by the oil prints of St. Sebastian on either side of them. Many of the realistic paintings demonstrated the young martyr as a delicate youth with fragile flesh. Kyle noticed that a few of the paintings depicted a yellow glow behind Sebastian's head. Although Kyle's brain was numb from the heroin, his inquisitiveness got the best of him. Kyle was aware that Jase could explain the symbolism. Jase always had an intelligent way about him, though he rarely put it to use.

"Hey," Kyle's voice eerily echoed throughout the cathedral. It didn't seem like his voice at all; it was as if the wave of sound had been slowed. At that point, Kyle knew the heroin had fully overtaken him. "Hey, Jase."

"What?" Jase called back, his full attention remaining on the crucifix.

"What's with all the gold circles around the guy's head?"

Jase was perturbed by the ridiculous question. He had no clue of what Kyle was speaking. Annoyed, Jase halted and turned to Kyle. "What are you talking about?"

"The paintings," Kyle pointed. "It looks like the guy in the paintings loves golden showers, eh?" Kyle couldn't help but chuckle, and his stomach folded from the laughter.

"You're stupid," said Jase. "We're in the St. Sebastian Cathedral and those are paintings of the saint. Artists paint gold circles around saints in their works; it represents them as martyrs."

"Excuse me; I didn't realize you were such the religious fanatic."

"I'm not, and I don't care about those. I'm here for one thing only," Jase stated as his eyes fell back to the crucified Christ. His hypnotic movement continued toward his obsession.

Kyle followed closely behind and observed the most common painting depicting St. Sebastian. The young man's hands were tied above him, and arrows pierced the tender flesh of his stomach and sides. Kyle gazed closer at one of the arrows and thought he saw a ruby droplet of blood run from the puncture wound. "I wonder if it hurt," he called out.

Jase ignored the comment and continued advancing toward the altar.

***

When Jase was eighteen, he made love to his identical twin.

Their mother was gone that day. She was working overtime at the office to have the extra money to pay for her sons' birthday gifts.

Jase (or Jason, as his mother would call him) had always been attracted to other boys at his high school. Although, he hadn't been intimate with another man until the week before, when he and Corey Chambers engaged in mutual masturbation after school one day in the Theatre Department. It was from this experience that Jase assumed that since he and his twin liked the same styles, foods, and pastimes, perhaps Mason wanted to share the experience of gay intimacy as well.

Mason strolled into Jase's bedroom, wearing a towel around his waist. His blond locks dripped water onto his chest. Jase looked up from his picture book of sculptures and noticed Mason's pectorals were slightly more developed than his own were. "Happy birthday, bro," Mason spoke.

Jase rose from the bed to greet his twin. "Happy birthday," he responded. Jase embraced Mason, hugging him tightly and feeling the water droplets soak through his cotton shirt. Jase didn't want to let go. It felt so exhilarating to feel another man's flesh against his—their chests evenly matched and pressed hard against each other, the clean-shaven softness of their cheeks side by side, and their full lips so close together.

Jase pulled back slightly, his arms still encircling Mason's broad back. He looked deep into his twin's hazel eyes, searching for a lustful spark that told him it was all right. Jase planted his mouth on Mason's and pushed his tongue past Mason's lips.

Mason immediately pulled back. His eyes bulged from the shock of Jase's kiss. "What are you doing, Jase?"

"It's all right," Jase said as he rubbed his hand up and down Mason's back in comfort. "I want to show you something. You're really going to like it."

"I don't know," Mason hesitated. "I don't think we should be doing this."

"Mason, nobody will know. Come on, it will be our secret birthday gift to each other. We'll always remember this. Besides, we're eighteen. We're men now and we can do what we want."

Mason didn't condone the idea, but he didn't refuse either. Instead, he allowed Jase to touch him; he let Jase run his hand over his chest, to his belly, and down to his semi-erect cock. Mason watched in amazement as Jase stripped the towel off him and got to his knees. Jase swallowed his twin's cock, and Mason became instantly hard. Ah the pleasure, as Mason fell into a world of euphoria. The tingling sensation in his testicles mounted and felt indescribable. Jase's mouth felt so good, and Mason's morals were no longer of consequence so long as Jase continued providing such sensations.

Jase stood up and undressed himself. He grabbed Mason and threw him on the bed. Mason saw Jase's own cock throbbing and noticed a feral, animalistic look in Jase's eyes. Jase flipped Mason over and rubbed his hands over the finely toned, half-orbs of Mason's buttocks. Reaching over to the bedside table and grabbing some lotion, Jase emptied a large amount into his hands and applied it to Mason's tight hole. He quickly slid two fingers in and out of Mason, heard him moan and yelp at the same time, then thrust his cock inside of his twin.

Mason could feel the lengthy shaft of his twin enter him from behind. He released a muffled scream into the pillow. The flaring pain surged throughout his entire body and his erection fell limp. Mason's resistance did nothing to stop Jase's incessant drive of his hips against his buttocks. Soon, Mason forced himself to relax and discovered a completely new sensation that caused him to grow hard once again. Now, with each of Jase's forceful thrusts, a delightful sensation ignited every nerve in his body with lusting gratification. A bubbling sensitivity crawled from the base of Mason's cock. He stridently groaned as he felt a warm liquid shoot from beneath him and splatter across his stomach.

Jase witnessed the satiated bellow of his twin's orgasm and it brought him to the brink of cumming. He drove deeper and faster into Mason until he collapsed onto his brother's back, spilling himself into his twin. His rushed breathing slowed as he pulled himself from out of Mason. "Happy birthday," he whispered as he kissed the nape of Mason's neck. Jase arose from the bed and made his way to the bathroom to towel himself off.

Mason rolled over and touched the creamy liquid that stained his stomach. He began to cry.

That was the last birthday Jase and Mason had shared.

***

Jase stood before the altar of St. Sebastian's Cathedral and studied the form of Christ crucified upon the cross. His mind swam with myriad fantasies of how he could seduce and make love to the sacred icon. If just to touch, if only to break Christ's lanky body as he fucked him.

Kyle slowly shook his head back and forth, amused by the tracing light from the candles that became a streaking blur. His thoughts were filled with mystery and wonder as he watched Jase's steady look upon the Christ image. The intensity of Jase's stare reminded him of when they made love. Kyle's loins were begging for action; he wanted to go to the club. Yet, in this sanctified place where angels and worshipers congregated, he experienced an unusual peace surround him. Everything felt great! His content reflections swirled in his brain and he was high as a kite. Jase's rapt gaze had Kyle feeling both scared and entertained. He broke the silence.

"So, this is the man of your dreams," he snickered.

"Yes, I want him so badly. I'm sure this is the exact size of the real Christ. Isn't he beautiful?" Jase appeared to be in a spellbinding trance.

Kyle gave credence to Jase's fantasy. "Go ahead, have him."

"I'm so fucking hard," Jase claimed.

Jase's statement teased Kyle. There would be no club tonight. There would be only he, Jase, the church, and Jase's fantasy. Kyle walked up from behind and wrapped his arms around Jase's stomach. "Have you ever fucked in a church…no, wait…have you ever fucked on heroin in a church?"

"No," Jase called back as he leaned back into Kyle's embrace.

"Come on," Kyle whispered as he pecked at Jase's neck, "let's live out your fantasy. Go for it." Kyle nudged Jase toward the captured image of Christ on the cross.

Jase's mind was hampered by lust and caprice as he reached upward to touch the foot of Christ. The texture was soft and warm, almost like human flesh, and felt nothing like that of a painted carving. Jase longed for the lithe body of Christ; he wanted Christ to kiss him, to touch him.

No sooner than his brain became flooded by such inhumane desires, did Jase's mouth fall open as he gaped into Christ's eyes. Kyle noticed the daunted expression upon his friend's face as he fixed his eyes upon the developing phenomena.

The dark irises of the model Jesus shifted and looked down upon the two men. His head moved from its craned position and fell forward as a grin ignited his face. The body of Christ began to buck against the cross to which he was secured. He opened his mouth wide and took in a deep breath as his chest expanded from the revitalizing oxygen. Christ prominently exhaled and took notice of each of his nailed hands. He slowly glanced down at his feet, overlapped and brought together by a single iron spike driven into his flesh that bonded him with the lower length of the cross. Christ boisterously roared in agony and despair. His thunderous screams bounced off the walls of St. Sebastian's cathedral.

Sweat beaded upon his tan flesh as droplets of blood crept down his brow from the crown of thorns that dug deep into his scalp. Christ forcefully pushed his body against the cross, his eyes welling with tears both clear and bloody. Like melting wax, his hands and feet effortlessly slid through the iron spikes, stretching the flesh like unending strings to a puppet, and jutted bloody fountains as he landed to the floor of St. Sebastian's. Free! He was free of the cross, and the first thing he did was eagerly grasp at the crown of thorns upon his head and throw it aside. Christ's hands, head, and feet expelled blood upon the marble floor and created a pool of crimson gore. He remained stock still as he keenly gazed at Jase and Kyle.

Surely, this was a dream! Undoubtedly, this was the hallucinogenic byproduct of the heroin. The yellow liquid had brought on these sacred phantasms, this nightmare fantastic, and Kyle would see it no other way. Yes, it was all illusion because he was the man of illusions. *Remember Travis?* his mind forced. No, this wasn't the death of a human, but the awakening of an inanimate thing. He would go with it, yes, because this was Jase's fantasy and he and Jase shared everything.

Was Jase experiencing the same fantasy, participating in the same drug-induced trip he was on? He must have been, because Jase was reaching out to touch Christ.

Jase's heart hammered from the fear and anticipation of touching Jesus. Oh, how fucking unbelievable, to touch the son of the God almighty! Jase reached up and slid his fingers against the grainy texture of Jesus' cheek. He brought his fingers to Christ's gritty lips before he moved inward and kissed them. Jase's tongue rushed into Christ's mouth and the surprisingly wet saliva that mingled with his own awakened a purity and anxiousness that reached out into every fiber of his body, detonating an ultimate sexual energy.

Behind Jase, Kyle gently kissed about the nape of his friend's neck and observed the thick, dark eyebrows of Christ as they arced and invited the red lines of blood that inched downward from the perforation along his hairline. The entire church spun circles around the threesome and Kyle became dizzy. Still, the image of Jase kissing Christ was facing Kyle. He maintained his position by pulling himself closer behind Jase. Kyle reached beyond Jase's shoulders and ran his fingers through Jesus' tangled, espresso hair. Along the sweating hairline of Christ, Kyle thought he felt lumps, but he disregarded it.

Pulling back from his deep kiss with Christ, Jase observed Kyle's hands combing Jesus' hair. He felt Kyle's body firmly against his backside and placed his hand upon Christ's chest. Jase moved his hand down the wet and sweaty surface of Christ's flesh, along the hollows of his concaved stomach, until he reached beneath his loincloth. What lay between his hands was the mystery of millennia. Jase fondled the crushed-velvet texture of Christ's limp cock. He curiously watched the insipid expression on Christ's face and Kyle's thumb moving over the growing lumps upon the sacrosanct man in front of him.

Kyle froze when he witnessed the lumps upon Christ's head come alive. This had to be a bad trip; it had to be some bad smack! Nevertheless, he pulled Jase's body close to him as the latest revelation came to pass. Jase was reluctant to fall into Kyle's arms and reached out to Christ.

The puncture wounds along Christ's scalp were replaced with bulblike lesions that surfaced from the deep, bloody holes. The pale red orbs pulsed and, soon, they jutted outward in wiry wavelike fashion. Emitting from Christ's head was a crown of slithering, snakelike limbs that flowingly shifted. There must have been a dozen, each where the thorns of his fateful crown had been placed. They rhythmically danced, their egg-formed heads bobbling back and forth, like musical antennae trying to contact Heaven.

Kyle attempted to scream for his friend to step back from the gruesome being toward which Jase drifted. *Jase! Get the fuck away from it!* he tried to holler. However, Kyle's voice had gone mute. He felt his lips mouth the words but could only hear them as a distant echo within his head.

Jase felt Christ's limp cock begin coiling around his hand. It circled his palm once, then his thumb, and his wrist. Like a boa constrictor, it continued tightly wrapping around Jase's wrist until Jase could view the blue circumcised head that pulsed and secreted an orange substance from the opening of the urethra. The jelly-like substance slowly crawled upward to Jase's bicep.

Jase was open-mouthed; his brain swam in a sea of confusion where both fear and pleasure swirled together in an undercurrent of astonishment. His own cock grew rigid; the heavy thud within his chest stifled his breathing. Jase's mouth salivated at the thought of licking at Christ's eccentric organ. As much as he wanted to bend his head downward, the coiling creature pulled at his arm and brought him closer to Christ. He wanted to itch at the orange slime that began to creep up his arm toward his shoulder. Jase watched arms reach out to clinch him, then closed his eyes.

Still embracing Jase from behind, Kyle felt himself being pulled forward with his friend. A prickly sensation infiltrated the skin of his hands and arms. Kyle tried to release his grip from Jase, but discovered his arms would not move. It was as it they were attached to one another by his hands. Itchy. Wet. Kyle observed the carroty substance come into view as it made its way over the clothing that deteriorated from Jase's shoulders. Kyle could feel Jase's warm back against his heaving chest. Their clothes had disintegrated into nothing, as if the orange gel contained a hidden acidity that melted away their garments but left their skin intact.

Kyle's panicked gaze met the eyes of Christ. Jesus' eyes flickered with tints of ginger as if his sclera were performing a stroboscopic dance to which the wiry snakes upon his forehead danced. Kyle bucked but was unable to move. He attempted another scream when he felt Christ's arms and legs anxiously wrap around both he and Jase. The bulbous snakelike tentacles raced over their heads. Jase could feel them slither down his naked back, over the curves of his buttocks, and encircling the trio.

Kyle placed his lips upon the nape of Jase's neck as he closed his eyes.

***

They drifted in a calming peace. The hollow thuds of their heartbeats sounded muffled and distant. Their bodies were cradled by heavy liquid, as if they twins within the womb of a relaxed mother. It was when both Jase and Kyle attempted to breathe that their eyelids shot open.

There was no air to breathe, only a thick watery substance that reflected bloody orange hues like that of a rotten pomegranate. Their naked bodies swam within their constricting shell, turning in graceful circles with bulged eyes that conveyed a silent language of dread and disbelief.

Just as Kyle made an attempt at swimming toward Jase, he stalled. From behind Jase, the nude Christ grappled onto him and thrust his cock into Jase's anus. They propelled forward, floating like angels in the clouds but with the unclean thoughts of devils. Jase's mouth widened and Kyle could only imagine what horrifying screams could emit from his friend had they not been muted by the syrupy liquid of their environment.

Kyle maneuvered his body to turn so that he could escape, but a tough wall of tight plasma greeted him. While frantically trying to push at the firm barrier and break free, Kyle felt the bodies of his friend and Christ crash against his back. He anxiously peered down to discover Jesus' arms and legs wrapping around his torso and legs, bringing the three of them into a fetal position. Kyle endeavored to gasp from the instant agony of feeling Jase's rigid cock being forced into his ass. Kyle felt the fingertips of Jesus' hand upon his testicles as Christ drove Jase within him.

Jase was trapped—in front of him, the back of his best friend; behind him, Jesus' chest pressed hard against him. Jase tried relaxing from the enormous shaft stuck inside of him. He allowed the muscles in his anus to conform to the monstrosity within him as he focused upon the oval structure in which they drifted. For a few seconds, Jase experienced an awkward tranquility.

Without warning, the trio consisting of Kyle, Jase, and Christ began spinning within their liquid surroundings. The three bodies horizontally rolled within the center of the structure to which they were imprisoned. Kyle tried freeing himself, but Jesus' arms and legs were locked around him, causing the trio to remain as one unholy threesome.

Butterflies screamed within Kyle and Jase's stomach, the vibrations from the giddiness tickling their chests and throats. Kyle and Jase were dizzy from the rotations, nauseous from seeing the unending curves of their oval prison passing above and below them. Orange and pink and red...rolling and spinning and constricted together...itchy gel massaging them and inside of them and being breathed in—of where was the end to such madness?

A hollow shriek infiltrated Kyle and Jase's environment, piercing their ears and causing their eyes to wince. "Sinner," it screeched.

Jase veritably fainted from the pain of Christ bucking his hips and driving his cock within him. He experienced the stabbing sensations of cold spikes growing inside him. It was as if barbs had grown all along the side of the organ that filled him. Christ made another thrust and Jase felt the small spears tear along the delicate area of his anal cavity. Jase had no choice but to force himself into Kyle. As pleasurable as it may have once been, there was no gratification in the act. Jase's anus flared with each drive of Christ's hips. His anus burned; it felt like an army of ants was crawling all over the strewn gore of his ass. Another thrust from Christ's hips and Jase's eyelids flickered. From his peripheral vision, he observed strewn pieces of bloodied flesh and slow squirming maggots make their way from behind.

***

Jase opened his eyes to a welcoming sight. His twin, Mason, stood naked before him. They were back at their childhood home. They were in their bedroom.

"Mason," Jase spoke, surprised and elated by the sound of his own voice. "I missed you so much, bro!"

Jase extended his arms to hug his twin, but Mason pushed his palms flat against Jase's chest.

"What's wrong, Mason?"

The look on Mason's face contained no expression. Jase watched as his twin opened his mouth wide.

"Mason?"

"SINNER!" a voice screeched from Mason's mouth, though his lips didn't form the word.

Jase took in an unnerving breath before the intake of his lungs was replaced by a pool of orange liquid that projected from Mason's mouth. Jase choked and gasped for air.

"SINNER!" The inhuman shriek pierced Jase's ears.

Jase hurried back from his brother. "Mason, no!" he screamed. The back of Jase's legs hit the corner of his childhood bed and he fell upon the soft mattress.

Jase trembled and tears flowed from his eyes as he watched his twin approach.

Jase cringed from his brother as he observed his twin pull at his hardened cock. His heartbeats were rapid and heavy as he watched Mason. His twin was touching his own shaft and pulling on it. Jase's eyes widened from his brother's cock being pulled six inches longer than it already had been. Jase recoiled as he horrifically studied the pliability of Mason's dick. His brother tugged and shaped it as a sculptor would clay. Mason took the mushroom-shaped head and stretched its ends and top into a three-sided point. Jase's twin had a short spear between his legs.

Jase tried to scurry to his feet, but Mason had already pinned him down and flipped him over with ungodly strength.

"No, Mason," Jase begged.

The shriek returned. "SINNER!" Jase felt the spear of his twin's cock impale his ass. Jase bawled as his insides seared. Every thrust of his brother had him crying out and screeching in agony.

"I'M SORRY," Jase bawled. "I'M SORRY!"

***

Kyle cringed with each drive of Jase's bucking hips. The combination of Jase's thrusts and Christ's limbs pulling him back amplified the aching sensation within his ass. Kyle closed his eyes as he fell into the sexual rhythm forced by the monstrosity of Jesus. With each flinch, Kyle prayed that Jase would finally orgasm. Perhaps, then, this nightmare would be over. To his dismay, Jase's hips continued to shove into him. In fact, Kyle began to feel a cold limpness pushing into his ass.

When Kyle opened his eyes, he was horridly welcomed by a slew of maggots and pieces of torn, bloodied flesh that seemed to pulse with their own life. He flinched back. It only pushed Jase's limp cock farther against the delicate wall of his anus. Although Kyle wanted to cry, the thick orange liquid saturated any possible tears.

From above him, Kyle noticed a movement of chocolate strands that stirred in the same slow motion as the maggots all around. It was hair! It was Christ's hair! Kyle kept his eyes rolled upward, straining them as he observed the strands of Jesus' hair grow longer. The locks of hair began discoloring, turning from their natural, dark brown color to that of a yellow chemical. Soon, the hair was reaching from above and on either side of him, flowing with the gracefulness of majestic eels. The yellowish strands of hair swelled in front of Kyle. Kyle wanted to close his eyes from what he saw next, but was unable to do so—such was the ghastly magnificence of what was transpiring.

The surrounding locks of Christ began shimmering and flashing with their yellowish hues. From the ends of the strands, silver needles began protruding. The needles stretched out from the end of each hair by six inches. *Oh fuck*, Kyle thought. His heart hesitantly hammered within his chest.

Kyle buckled, but it was to no avail. The first needle entered the crook of his right arm. He glanced in terror as it was inserted half way. He watched in astonishment as the yellow substance seeped from the hair of Christ and into his veins. Afterward, the lock of hair went back to its natural color. It was if the strands of Jesus' hair were slim hypodermics filled with heroin, emptying into Kyle's veins.

Another needle pushed itself into Kyle's groin. Then another jabbed itself in the space between his toes. A suffocating tightness filled Kyle's chest. Everything around him went gray and his vision had him seeing triple. Kyle felt like laughing, but then the next needle entered his neck and he thought he would explode. Before his eyes rolled into the back of his head, he witnessed four more needles approaching his sight.

***

Travis greeted Kyle. Kyle quickly sat up and looked the young man up and down as if he a long lost friend.

"Travis? But how?"

Travis bent down and lapped at Kyle's chest, licked at his hardening nipples.

Kyle felt himself growing hard, and chalked the terror of what he had just experienced to a drug-induced nightmare.

"Hey, Travis." Kyle smiled. He pulled Travis' head from his chest and stared him in the eyes. God, look at those fucking blue eyes! Oh, how he needed him here and now!

Travis stared at him, unyielding a smile.

"We're going to fly to the stars tonight, my Travis. Remember, I'm your man of illusions? Oh, and I have something for you." Kyle reached into his jacket pocket. He searched for the prepared hypodermic but couldn't find it. Where the fuck was it?

Kyle looked back to Travis, strangely taken by the way the youthful man had his mouth open wide. "Listen," Kyle explained, "I can't let you blow me until I find my..."

"SINNER!" an ungodly voice shrieked and infiltrated the night.

Kyle balked and scanned the immediate area. He returned his attention to Travis whose mouth was still wide-open. "I don't know what the fuck is going on but I think we should—"

Kyle was cut off by the orange vomit that exploded from Travis mouth and splashed all over his face. Kyle gagged and placed his hands to his head, wiping at the jelly gore. "What the fuck, Travis?"

Once Travis was back in Kyle's vision, Kyle tried to turn and run from the atrocity that stood before him. However, Travis grabbed at his leg and brought Kyle flat to his back upon the asphalt of the alley. Kyle was helpless from Travis' strength that pinned him. All that Kyle could do was watch the terror play out before him.

Travis arched his back, exposing his canine teeth to the light of the moon. The silvery tips of needles protruded from both teeth. From either end, heroin dripped in its dirty yellow-colored fashion.

"Please no," Kyle pleaded.

Travis bent in toward Kyle's neck like a vampire in need of sustenance.

Kyle experienced the sharp points of the needles burrow beneath the tender flesh of his neck. In a matter of seconds, Kyle's surroundings appeared cloudy. He floated, yet the once gleaming stars above seemed blurry and farther away. He wildly shook his head left and right, trying to shake the drugs from his veins. "No, no, no, no, no," Kyle repeated in a half-daze.

"SINNER!" the voice cracked the night once again.

In his haste to rid this wanton chaos within a nightmare, Kyle found Travis' stare. The silvery gleam in Travis' eyes produced two more needles that slowly ejected from Travis' pupils. "PLEASE," Kyle screamed.

Travis head came down, eyes locking eyes, as if it a passionate kiss.

Kyle's eyes watered from the penetration of the needles. As much as he wanted to close his eyes, Kyle knew his eyelids would be sliced by the razor sharpness protruding from Travis' sapphires.

"I didn't mean to," Kyle whimpered.

Soon, darkness smothered his sight.

***

The bulky doors of St. Sebastian's Cathedral swung inward as Father Hastings walked in. His mind raced with anxiousness at recalling which maintenance worker had left the doors unlocked. Father Hastings peered to the left and right, studying the gleaming varnish of the pews, before he noticed the atrocity before the altar of Christ.

Father Hastings sprinted down the center aisle of the church and came to a halt six feet from the scene that lay before him. He gasped and put his hand to his mouth. Right away, he gestured the Sign of the Cross over his torso. Father Hastings grabbed a handkerchief from his right pocket to mask the pungent odor.

The sight that lay before him was that of two naked, young men. Their bodies appeared lifeless and were covered in an orange substance. Upon the floor, the liquid was mixed with pools of shit and blood.

"Dear God," the priest's voice echoed throughout the empty church.

Father Hastings looked up to the gigantic cross above the altar. Immediately, he pinpointed a small spot on the foot of the Christ statue. He walked around the bodies of the young men and to the cross. Staring in disgust, Father Hastings wiped off the maggot that squirmed upon Jesus Christ's crucified foot.

Andrew Wolter is the author of the novel *Nightfall*. Currently, he lives and creates within the metropolitan area of Phoenix, Arizona, amidst the stucco and glass that surround his environment. While his writing blurs (and tends to push) genre boundaries, Andrew feels there is always a place for darkness in any work of art. *Much of Madness, More of Sin* is his first short story collection. Andrew is currently working on his next novel. Visit Andrew Wolter on the web at www.AndrewWolter.com.

www.ingramcontent.com/pod-product-compliance
Lightning Source LLC
Chambersburg PA
CBHW020620250626
47154CB00004B/1600